THE HOTEL MAJESTIC

One of the most significant figures in twentieth-century European literature, GEORGES JOSEPH CHRISTIAN SIMENON was born on February 12, 1903, in Liège, Belgium. He began work as a reporter for a local newspaper at the age of sixteen, and at nineteen moved to Paris to embark on a career as a novelist. According to Simenon, the character Jules Maigret came to him one afternoon in a café in the small Dutch port of Delfzijl as he wrestled with writing a different sort of detective story. By noon the following day, he claimed, he had completed the first chapter of *Pietr-le-Letton, The Strange Case of Peter the Lett.* The pipe-smoking Commissaire Maigret would go on to feature in 75 novels and 28 stories, with estimated international sales to date of 850 million copies. His books have been translated into more than 50 languages.

The dark realism of Simenon's fiction has lent itself naturally to film adaptation with more than five hundred hours of television drama and sixty motion pictures produced throughout the world. A dazzling array of directors have tackled Simenon on screen, including Jean Renoir, Marcel Carné, Claude Chabrol, and Bertrand Tavernier. Maigret has been portrayed on film by Jean Gabin, Charles Laughton, and Pierre Renoir; and on television by Bruno Cremer, Rupert Davies, and, most recently, Michael Gambon.

Simenon died in 1989 in Lausanne, Switzerland, where he had lived for the latter part of his life.

For Nobel Laureate Andr̲

the greatest novelist" of twent̲

admirers outside of France incl̲

Gabriel García Márquez.

GEORGES SIMENON

THE HOTEL MAJESTIC

TRANSLATED BY
DAVID WATSON

PENGUIN BOOKS

PENGUIN BOOKS

Published by the Penguin Group

Penguin Group (USA) Inc., 375 Hudson Street, New York, New York 10014, U.S.A.
Penguin Group (Canada), 90 Eglinton Avenue East, Suite 700, Toronto,
Ontario, Canada M4P 2Y3 (a division of Pearson Penguin Canada Inc.)
Penguin Books Ltd, 80 Strand, London WC2R 0RL, England
Penguin Ireland, 25 St. Stephen's Green, Dublin 2, Ireland
(a division of Penguin Books Ltd)
Penguin Group (Australia), 250 Camberwell Road, Camberwell,
Victoria 3124, Australia (a division of Pearson Australia Group Pty Ltd)
Penguin Books India Pvt Ltd, 11 Community Centre,
Panchsheel Park, New Delhi – 110 017, India
Penguin Group (NZ), cnr Airborne and Rosedale Roads, Albany,
Auckland 1310, New Zealand (a division of Pearson New Zealand Ltd)
Penguin Books (South Africa) (Pty) Ltd, 24 Sturdee Avenue,
Rosebank, Johannesburg 2196, South Africa

Penguin Books Ltd, Registered Offices:
80 Strand, London WC2R 0RL, England

Maigret et les caves du Majestic first published 1942
This translation first published by Hamish Hamilton 1977
Published in Penguin Books 1982
Reissued under the present title with minor revisions in Penguin Classics 2003
This edition published in Penguin Books (USA) 2007

3 5 7 9 10 8 6 4 2

Copyright, Georges Simenon Limited, a Chorion Company, 1942
Translation copyright © Georges Simenon Limited, a Chorion Company, 1977
All rights reserved

LIBRARY OF CONGRESS CATALOGING IN PUBLICATION DATA
Simenon, Georges, 1903–1989.
[Caves du Majestic. English]
The Hotel Majestic / by Georges Simenon.
p. cm.
ISBN 978-0-14-303845-0
1. Maigret, Jules (Fictitious character)—Fiction. 2. Police—France—Paris—
Fiction I. Title.
PQ2637.I53C3813 2007
843'.912—dc22 2006050696

Printed in the United States of America

CONTENTS

PROSPER DONGE'S PUNCTURE

A car door slamming. The first thing he heard each day. The engine ticking over outside. Charlotte was probably saying goodbye to the driver? Then the taxi drove off. Footsteps. The sound of the key in the lock and the click of the electric light switch.

A match being struck in the kitchen and the slow "pfffttt" as the gas came alight.

Charlotte climbed slowly up the newly built staircase, having been on her feet all night. She crept noiselessly into the room. Another light switch. The light came on, a pink handkerchief with wooden tassels at the corners making a makeshift shade.

Prosper Donge kept his eyes firmly closed. Charlotte undressed, glancing at herself in the wardrobe mirror. When she got to her bra and girdle, she sighed. She was as plump and pink as a Rubens, but had a passion for constricting herself. When she had finished undressing, she rubbed the marks on her skin.

She had an irritating way of getting into the bed, kneeling on it first so that the mattress dipped to one side.

"Your turn, Prosper!"

He got up. She dived quickly into the warm hollow he had left, pulled the bedcovers up to her eyes and lay there unmoving.

"Is it raining?" he asked, running water into the basin.

A muffled groan. It didn't matter. The water was icy to shave in. Trains rumbled past below.

Prosper Donge got dressed. Charlotte sighed from time to time because she couldn't get to sleep with the light on. Just as he stretched out his right hand to the switch, with his other hand already on the doorknob, she muttered thickly: "Don't forget to go and pay the money for the wireless."

There was hot coffee on the stove—too hot. He drank it standing up. Then, with the gestures of someone who does the same things every day, at the same time, he wrapped a knitted scarf round his neck, and put on his hat and coat.

Finally he wheeled his bicycle along the passage and out of the door.

The air was always damp and cold at that hour of the morning, and the pavements were wet although it hadn't rained; the people sleeping behind their closed shutters would probably waken to a warm, sunny day.

The street, with detached houses and little gardens on either side, ran steeply downhill. There was an occasional glimpse, through the trees, of the lights of Paris far down below.

It was no longer dark. But it wasn't yet light. The sky was bluish mauve. Lights came on in a few windows and Prosper Donge braked sharply as he reached the level crossing which was shut and which he crossed by the side gates.

After the Pont de Saint-Cloud, he turned left. A tug with its chain of barges was whistling angrily to be allowed into the lock.

The Bois de Boulogne . . . Lakes reflecting a whiter sky, with swans stirring awake . . .

As he reached the Porte Dauphine, Donge suddenly felt the ground become harder under his wheels. He went on a few metres, jumped off and saw that his back tyre was punctured.

He checked the time by his watch. It was ten to six. He began to walk quickly, pushing his bike, and his breath hung in the air as he panted along, with a burning sensation in his chest from the effort.

Avenue Foch . . . The shutters of the private houses were all still closed . . . Only an officer trotting along the ride followed by his orderly . . .

Getting lighter behind the Arc de Triomphe . . . He was hurrying along . . . getting very hot now . . .

Just at the corner of the Champs-Élysées, a policeman in a cape, near the newspaper kiosk, called out: "Puncture?"

He nodded. Only three hundred metres more. The Hotel Majestic, on the left, with all its windows still shuttered. The street lamps barely shed any light now.

He turned up the Rue de Berri, then the Rue de Ponthieu. There was a little bar open. And two houses farther along, a door which passers-by never noticed, the back entrance of the Majestic.

A man was coming out. He appeared to be in evening dress under his grey overcoat. He was bareheaded. His hair was plastered down and Prosper Donge thought it was Zebio, the dancer.

He could have glanced into the bar to see if he was right, but it didn't occur to him to do so. Still pushing his bike, he started down the long grey corridor, lit by a single light. He stopped at the clocking-on machine, turned the wheel, and put a card in at his number, 67, his eyes on the little clock which said ten past six. Click.

It was now established that he had arrived at the Majestic at 6:10 a.m.—ten minutes later than usual.

———

That was the official statement made by Prosper Donge, still-room chef at the big Champs-Élysées hotel.

He had continued to behave, he said, as on any other morning.

At that hour, the great basement with its twisting corridors, innumerable doors and grey-painted walls like those of a ship's gangway, was deserted. Here and there you could see a feeble light from a yellowish bulb, which was all the light there was at night, shining through the glass partitions.

There were glass partitions everywhere, with the kitchens on the left, and the pastrycook's kitchen beyond. Opposite was the room called the guests' servants' hall, where the senior staff and guests' private servants, chambermaids and chauffeurs ate. Then farther on, the junior staff dining-room, with long wooden tables and benches like school benches.

Finally, overlooking the basement like the bridge of a ship, a smaller glass cage, where the bookkeeper kept a check on everything which left the kitchens.

As he opened the door of the still-room, Prosper Donge had the impression that someone was going up the narrow staircase which led to the upper floors, but he didn't pay any attention to the fact. Or so he stated later.

He struck a match, just as Charlotte had done in their little house, and the gas went "pfffttt" under the smallest percolator, which he heated first for the few guests who got up early.

Only when he had done this did he go to the cloakroom. It was a fairly large room, down one of the corridors. There were several basins, a greyish mirror, and tall, narrow metal lockers round the walls, each with a number.

He opened locker 67 with his key. Took off his coat, hat and scarf. He changed his shoes because he liked wearing softer, elastic-sided shoes during the daytime. He put on a white jacket.

A few minutes to go . . . At half past six, the basement burst into life . . .

Upstairs, they were all still asleep, except the night porter, who was waiting to be relieved in the deserted foyer.

The percolator whistled. Donge filled a cup with coffee and started up the staircase, which was like one of those mysterious staircases in the wings of a theatre which lead to the most unexpected places.

Pushing open a narrow door, he found himself in the cloakroom in the foyer; no one would have known the door, covered by a large mirror, was there.

"Coffee!" he announced, putting the cup on the cloakroom counter. "All right?"

"OK!" the night porter grunted, coming to get it.

Donge went downstairs again. His three women helpers, the Three Fatties as they were called, had arrived. They were rough types, all three ugly—and one of them old and cantankerous. They were already noisily clanking cups and saucers in the sink.

Donge continued his daily routine, ranging the silver coffee pots in order of size—one, two or three cups . . . Then the little milk jugs . . . teapots . . .

He caught sight of Jean Ramuel, looking dishevelled, in the bookkeeper's glass booth.

"Hmm . . . Spent the night here again!" he said to himself.

For the past three or four nights, Ramuel, the bookkeeper, had slept at the hotel instead of going home to Montparnasse.

Officially, this was not allowed. There was a room with three or four beds in it at the end of the corridor, near the door leading to the wine cellars. But in theory the beds were for the use of members of the staff who needed to rest between their hours of work.

Donge waved his hand in greeting to Ramuel, who replied equally casually.

Then it was time for the head chef—vast and full of pomp—to arrive back from the market with his van which he parked in the Rue de Ponthieu for his assistants to unload.

By half past seven there were at least thirty people scurrying about in the basements of the Majestic, and bells began to ring, service-lifts began to descend and were loaded before ascending with their trays, while Ramuel speared pink, blue and white chits on the metal prongs on his desk.

Then it was time for the day porter, in his light blue uniform, to take up his post in the foyer, and for the post clerk to sort the letters in his little cubbyhole. The sun was probably shining out in the Champs-Élysées, but down in the basement they were only aware of the buses rumbling overhead, making the glass partitions tremble.

At a few minutes past nine—at four minutes past nine precisely, it was later established—Prosper Donge came out of his still-room and a few seconds later went into the cloakroom.

"I had left my handkerchief in my coat pocket . . ." he stated when interrogated.

At all events he found himself alone in the room with its hundred metal lockers. Did he open his? There were no witnesses. Did he look for his handkerchief? Possibly he did.

There were in fact not a hundred but only ninety-two lockers, all numbered. The last five were empty.

Why did it occur to Prosper Donge to open locker 89, which didn't belong to anyone and was therefore not locked?

"It was automatic . . ." he said later. "The door was ajar . . . I didn't think . . ."

In the locker was a body which had been pushed in upright and which had fallen over on itself. It was the body of a woman of about thirty, very blonde—peroxide blonde in fact—wearing a dress of fine black wool.

Donge didn't cry out. He turned very pale, and going up to Ramuel's glass cage, bent to whisper through the grille.

"Come here a minute . . ."

The bookkeeper followed him.

"Stay here . . . Don't let anyone in . . ."

Ramuel bounded up the stairs, burst into the foyer cloakroom and saw the porter talking to a chauffeur.

"Is the manager here yet?"

The porter gestured with his chin towards the manager's office.

———

Maigret paused outside the revolving door, and was about to tap his pipe on his heel to empty it. Then he shrugged and put it back in his mouth. It was his first pipe of the day—the best.

"The manager is expecting you, superintendent . . ."

There were few signs of life in the foyer as yet. An Englishman was arguing with the post clerk and a young girl walked through on grasshopper-long legs carrying a hatbox which she had probably come to deliver.

Maigret went into the office and the manager shook his hand silently and pointed to a chair. There was a green curtain across the glass door, but if one pulled it back a little one could see everything that went on.

"A cigar?"

"No thank you . . ."

They had known each other for a long time. There was no need to say much. The manager was wearing striped trousers, a black jacket and a tie which seemed to have been cut from some rigid material.

"Here . . ."

He pushed a registration form towards his visitor.

OSWALD J. CLARK, INDUSTRIALIST, OF DETROIT, MICHIGAN USA. TRAVELLING FROM DETROIT.

ARRIVED ON 12 FEBRUARY.

ACCOMPANIED BY: MRS. CLARK, HIS WIFE; TEDDY CLARK, AGED 7, HIS SON; ELLEN DARROMAN, AGED 24, GOVERNESS; GERTRUD BORMS, AGED 42, MAID.

SUITE 203.

The telephone rang. The manager answered impatiently. Maigret folded the form in four and put it in his wallet.

"Which of them is it?"

"Mrs. Clark . . ."

"Ah!"

"The hotel doctor, whom I telephoned as soon as I had informed the Police, and who lives just round the corner in the Rue de Berri, is already here. He says Mrs. Clark was strangled some time between 6 and 6:30 a.m."

The manager was plunged in gloom. There was no
need to tell an old hand like Maigret that it was a disaster
for the hotel and that if there was any way of hushing
it up . . .

"The Clark family have been here a week then . . ."
murmured the superintendent. "What sort of people are
they?"

"Well heeled . . . Very . . . He's a great, tall, silent American, about forty . . . Forty-five perhaps . . . His wife—
poor thing!—seems to be French . . . Twenty-eight or
nine . . . I didn't see very much of her . . . The governess is
pretty . . . The maid, who also looks after the child, is very
ordinary, rather surly . . . Ah! . . . I nearly forgot to tell
you . . . Clark left for Rome yesterday morning . . ."

"Alone?"

"From what I can gather, he is in Europe on business . . . He has a ball-bearing factory . . . He has to visit
various European capitals and he decided to leave his
wife, son and staff in Paris for the time being . . ."

"What train did he get?" Maigret asked.

The manager picked up the telephone.

"Hello! Porter? . . . What train did Mr. Clark catch yesterday . . . Suite 203, yes . . . Wasn't there any luggage to go
to the station? He only took a grip? . . . By taxi? . . . Désiré's
taxi? . . . Thank you . . .

"Did you get that, superintendent? He left at eleven
o'clock yesterday morning in a taxi, Désiré's taxi, which is
nearly always parked outside the hotel. He took only one
small bag with him . . ."

"Do you mind if I make a call myself? . . . Hello! Judicial
Police, please, mademoiselle . . . Police Headquarters? . . .
Lucas? Get over to the Gare de Lyon . . . Check on the
trains to Rome from 11 a.m. yesterday . . ."

He continued giving instructions, while his pipe
went out.

"Tell Torrence to find Désiré's taxi . . . Yes . . . Which is
usually outside the Majestic . . . Find out where he took a
fare, a tall thin American he picked up outside the hotel
yesterday . . . That's it . . ."

He looked for an ashtray in which to empty his pipe.
The manager handed him one.

"Are you sure you won't have a cigar? . . . The nanny is
in a great state . . . I thought it best to tell her . . . And the
governess didn't sleep at the hotel last night . . ."

"What floor is the suite on?"

"On the second floor . . . Looking out over the Champs-
Élysées . . . Mr. Clark's room, separated from his wife's by
a sitting-room . . . Then the child's room, the nanny's and
the governess's . . . They wanted to be all together . . ."

"Has the night porter left?"

"He can be reached by telephone, I know, because I had
to contact him one day. His wife is the concierge at a new
block of flats in Neuilly . . . Hello! . . . Can you get me . . ."

Five minutes later they knew that Mrs. Clark had gone
to the theatre alone the evening before, and that she had
got back a few minutes past midnight. The nanny had not
gone out. The governess on the other hand had not dined
at the hotel and had been out all night.

"Shall we go downstairs and have a look?" Maigret sighed.

The foyer was busier now, but no one had any idea of the drama which had taken place while they were still asleep.

"We'll go this way . . . I'll lead the way, superintendent . . ."

As he spoke, the manager frowned. Someone was coming through the revolving door, letting in a shaft of sunlight. A young woman in a grey suit came in and, as she passed the post desk, asked in English: "Anything for me?"

"That's her, superintendent—Miss Ellen Darroman . . ."

Fine silk stockings, with straight seams. The well-groomed look of someone who had dressed with care. She didn't look at all tired, and the brisk February air had brought colour to her cheeks.

"Do you want to talk to her?"

"Not yet . . . Wait a minute . . ."

And Maigret went over to an inspector he had brought with him, who was standing in a corner of the foyer.

"Don't let that girl out of your sight . . . If she goes into her room, stand outside the door . . ."

The cloakroom. The tall mirror turned on its hinges. The superintendent followed the manager down the narrow staircase. A sudden end to all the gilt, potted plants and elegant bustle. A smell of cooking rose to meet them.

"Does this staircase go to all the floors?"

"There are two of them . . . leading from the cellar to the attics . . . But you have to know your way around to use them . . . For instance, upstairs, there are little doors exactly the same as the other doors, but with no number on. None of the visitors would ever guess . . ."

It was nearly eleven o'clock. There were not fifty, but more like a hundred and fifty people now, scurrying about in the basement, some in cooks' white hats, others in waiters' coats, or cellarmen's aprons, and the women, like Prosper Donge's Three Fatties, doing the rough work . . .

"This way . . . Careful you don't get dirty or slip . . . The passages are very narrow . . ."

Through the glass partitions everyone stared at them, and particularly at the superintendent. Jean Ramuel was busy catching each chit handed up to him as its bearer flew past, and casting an eagle eye over the contents of the trays.

It was a shock to see the unexpected figure of a policeman standing on guard outside the cloakroom. The doctor—who was very young—had been warned that Maigret was coming, and was smoking a cigarette while waiting.

"Shut the door . . ."

The body was lying on the floor in the middle of the room, surrounded by the metal lockers. The doctor, still smoking, muttered: "She must have been attacked from behind . . . She didn't struggle for very long . . ."

"And her body wasn't dragged along the ground!" Maigret added, examining the dead woman's black clothes. "There are no traces of dust . . . Either the crime was committed here, or she was carried, by two people probably, because it would be difficult in this labyrinth of narrow corridors . . ."

There was a crocodile handbag in the locker in which she had been found. The superintendent opened it, and took out an automatic, which he slipped into his pocket, after checking the safety catch was on. There was nothing else in the bag except a handkerchief, a powder compact, and a few banknotes amounting to less than a thousand francs.

Behind them the basement was humming like a bee-hive. The service-lifts shot up and down, bells rang cease-lessly and they could see heavy copper saucepans being wielded behind the glass partitions of the kitchens, and chickens being roasted in their dozens.

"Everything must be left in place for the Public Pros-ecutor's Department to see," Maigret said. "Who found the body? . . ."

Prosper Donge, who was cleaning a percolator, was pointed out to him. He was tall, with the kind of red hair usually referred to as carroty, and looked about forty-five to forty-eight. He had blue eyes and his face was badly pockmarked.

"Has he been here long?"

"Five years . . . Before that he was at the Miramar, in Cannes . . ."

"Reliable?"

"Extremely reliable . . ."

There was a partition separating Donge and the super-intendent. Their eyes met through the glass. And a rush of colour flooded the face of the still-room chef, who like all redheads, had sensitive skin.

"Excuse me, sir . . . Superintendent Maigret is wanted on the telephone . . ."

It was Jean Ramuel, the bookkeeper, who had hurried out of his cage.

"If you'd like to take the call here—"

A message from Headquarters. There had only been two express trains to Rome since eleven o'clock the day before. Oswald J. Clark had not travelled on either of them. And the taxi driver, Désiré, whom they had managed to contact on the telephone at a bistro where he was one of the regulars, swore he had taken his fare, the day before, to the Hotel Aiglon, in the Boulevard Montparnasse.

Voices, from the staircase, one of them the high-pitched voice of a young woman protesting in English to a room waiter who was trying to bar her way.

It was the governess, Ellen Darroman, who was bearing down on them.

2

MAIGRET GOES BICYCLING

Pipe in mouth, bowler on the back of his head, and hands in the pockets of his vast overcoat with the famous velvet collar, Maigret watched her arguing vehemently with the hotel manager.

And one glance at the superintendent's face made it clear that there would not be much sympathy lost between him and Ellen Darroman.

"What's she saying?" he sighed, interrupting, unable to understand a single word the American woman said.

"She wants to know if it's true Mrs. Clark has been murdered, and if anyone has telephoned to Rome to let Oswald J. Clark know; she wants to know where the body has been taken and if . . ."

But the girl didn't let him finish. She had listened impatiently, frowning, had thrown Maigret a cold glance and had gone on talking faster than ever.

"What's she saying?"

"She wants me to show her the body and . . ."

Maigret gently took the American girl's arm, to guide her towards the cloakroom. But he knew she would shy away from the contact. Just the kind of woman who exas-

perated him in American films! A terrifyingly brisk walk.
All the kitchen staff were gaping at her through the glass
partitions.

"Do come in," murmured the superintendent, not without irony.

She took three steps forward, saw the body wrapped
in a blanket on the floor, remained stock still and started
jabbering away in English again.

"What's she saying?"

"She wants us to uncover the body . . ."

Maigret complied, without taking his eyes off her. He
saw her start, then immediately recover her composure in
spite of the horrifying nature of what she saw.

"Ask her if she recognizes Mrs. Clark . . ."

A shrug. A particularly disagreeable way of tapping
her high heel on the floor.

"What's she saying?"

"That you know as well as she does."

"In that case, please ask her to go up to your office and
tell her that I have a few questions to ask her."

The manager translated. Maigret took the opportunity
of covering the dead woman's face again.

"What's she saying?"

"She says 'no.'"

"Really? Kindly inform her of my position as head of
the Special Squad of the Judicial Police . . ."

Ellen, who was looking straight at him, spoke without
waiting for this to be translated. And Maigret repeated his
interminable: "What's she saying?"

"*What's she saying?*" she repeated, imitating him, over-come by unjustifiable irritation.

And she spoke in English again, as if to herself.

"Translate what she's saying for me, will you?"

"She says that . . . that she knows perfectly well you're from the police . . . that . . ."

"Don't be afraid!"

"That one only has to see you with your hat on and your pipe in your mouth . . . I'm so sorry . . . You wanted me to tell you . . . She says she won't go up to my office and that she won't answer your questions . . ."

"Why not?"

"I'll ask her . . ."

Ellen Darroman, who was lighting a cigarette, listened to the manager's question, shrugged again and snapped a few words.

"She says she's not under any obligation to answer and that she will only obey an official summons . . ."

At which the girl threw a last look at Maigret, turned on her heel and walked, with the same decisive air, towards the staircase.

The manager turned somewhat anxiously towards the superintendent, and was amazed to see that he was smiling.

————

He had had to take off his overcoat, because of the heat in the basement, but he hadn't abandoned his bowler or his pipe. Thus accoutred, he wandered peacefully along the corridors, with his hands behind his back, stopping from time to time by one of the glass partitions, rather as if he were inspecting an aquarium.

The huge basement, with its electric lights burning all day long, did in fact strike him as being very like an oceano-graphical museum. In each glass cage there were creatures, varying in number, darting to and fro. You could see them constantly appearing and disappearing, heavily laden, car-rying saucepans or piles of plates, setting service-lifts or goods-lifts in motion, forever using the little instruments which were the telephones.

"What would someone from another planet make of it all? . . ."

The visit from the DPP had only lasted a few minutes, and the examining magistrate had given Maigret a free hand as usual. The latter had made several telephone calls from Jean Ramuel's bookkeeper's cage.

Ramuel's nose was set so crookedly, that one always seemed to be seeing him in profile. And he looked as though he was suffering from a liver complaint. When his lunch was brought to him on a tray, he took a sachet of white powder from his waistcoat pocket and dissolved it in a glass of water.

Between one and three o'clock, the pace was at its most hectic, everything happening so fast that it was like seeing a film run off in fast motion.

"Excuse me . . . Sorry . . ."

People were constantly bumping into the superintend-ent, who continued his walk unperturbed, stopping and starting, asking a question now and then.

How many people had he talked to? At least twenty, he reckoned. The head chef had explained to him how the kitchens were run. Jean Ramuel had told him what the different coloured slips of paper meant.

And he had watched—still through the glass partitions—the guests' servants having their lunch. Gertrud Borms, the Clarks' nanny, had come down. A large, hard-faced woman.

"Does she speak French?"

"Not a word . . ."

She had eaten heartily, chatting to a liveried chauffeur who sat opposite her.

But what amazed him most of all was the sight of Prosper Donge, all this while, in his still-room. He looked exactly like a large goldfish in its bowl. His hair was a fiery red. He had the almost brick-red complexion redheads sometimes have, and his lips were thick and fish-like.

And he looked exactly like a fish when he came to press his face up against the glass, with his great, round, bewildered eyes, probably worried because the superintendent hadn't spoken to him yet.

Maigret had questioned everyone. But he had hardly seemed to notice Prosper Donge's presence, although it was he who had discovered the body, and he was therefore the principal witness.

Donge, too, had his lunch, on a little table in his still-room, while his three women bustled round him. A bell would ring about once a minute to indicate that the service-lift was coming down. It arrived at a sort of hatch. Donge seized the slip of paper on it, and replaced it with the order on a tray, and the lift went up again to one of the upper floors.

All these seemingly complicated operations were in fact quite simple. The large dining-room of the Majestic, where two or three hundred people would then be having lunch, was immediately over the kitchens, so most of the service-lifts went there. Each time one of them came down again, the sound of music was wafted down with it.

Some of the guests had their meals in their rooms, however, and there was a waiter on each floor. There was also a grill-room on the same floor as the basement, where there was dancing in the afternoons from about five o'clock.

The men from the Forensic Laboratory had come for the body, and two specialists from the Criminal Records Office had spent half an hour working on locker 89 with cameras and powerful lights, looking for fingerprints.

None of this seemed to interest Maigret. They would be sure to inform him of the result in due course.

Looking at him, you would have thought he was making an amateurish study of how a grand hotel functions. He went up the narrow staircase, opened a door, then immediately closed it again, because it led to the large dining-room, which was filled with the sound of clinking cutlery, music and conversation.

He went up to the next floor. A corridor, with doors numbered to infinity and a red carpet stretching into the distance.

It was clear that any of the guests could open the door and make their way to the basement. It was the same as

with the entrance in the Rue de Ponthieu. Two car attendants, a porter, and commissionaires guarded the revolving door leading from the Champs-Élysées, but any stray
passer-by could get into the Majestic by using the staff
entrance and no one would probably have noticed he was
there.

It is the same with most theatres. They are rigidly
guarded at the front, but wide open on the stage-door side.

From time to time people went into the cloakroom in
their working clothes. Shortly afterwards they could be
seen leaving, smartly dressed, in their hats and coats.

They were going off duty. The head chef went to the
back room for a nap, which he did every day between the
lunch and dinner shifts.

Soon after four there was a loud burst of music from
near at hand in the grill-room, and the dancing began.
Prosper Donge, looking exhausted, filled rows of minute
teapots, and microscopic milk jugs, and then came anxiously up to the glass partition once more, casting nervous
glances in Maigret's direction.

At five o'clock his three women went off duty and were
replaced by two others. At six he took a wad of bills and
a sheet of paper, which was obviously his accounts for
the day, to Jean Ramuel. Then he in turn went into the
cloakroom, came out in his street clothes and fetched his
bicycle, the puncture having been repaired by one of the
bellboys.

Outside it was now dark. The Rue de Ponthieu was
congested. Prosper Donge made for the Champs-Élysées,

weaving his way between taxis and buses. When he was almost at the Étoile, he suddenly did an about-turn, bicycled back to the Rue de Ponthieu, and went into a radio shop, where he handed over three hundred odd francs to the cashier as one of the monthly instalments which he had contracted to pay.

Back to the Champs-Élysées. Then on to the regal calm of the Avenue Foch, with only the occasional car gliding silently past. He pedalled slowly, with the air of one who has a long way to go yet—an honest citizen pedalling along the same route at the same time every day.

A voice from behind, speaking quite close to him: "I hope you don't mind, Monsieur Donge, if I go the rest of the way with you?"

He braked so violently that he skidded and almost collided with Maigret on his bicycle. For it was Maigret who was bicycling along beside him, on a bike which was too small for him, which he had borrowed from a bellboy at the Majestic.

"I can't think," Maigret continued, "why everyone who lives in the suburbs doesn't go by bicycle. It's so much more healthy and agreeable than going by bus or train!"

They were entering the Bois de Boulogne. Soon they saw the shimmer of street-lights reflected in the lake.

"You were so busy all day that I didn't like to disturb you in your work . . ."

And Maigret, too, was pedalling along with the regular rhythm of someone who is used to bicycling. Now and then there was the click of a gear.

"Do you know what Jean Ramuel did before he came to the Majestic?"

"He was a bank accountant . . . The Atoum Bank, in the Rue Caumartin . . ."

"Hmm! . . . The Atoum Bank . . . Doesn't sound too good to me . . . Don't you think he has rather a shifty look about him?"

"He's not very well . . ." Prosper Donge mumbled.

"Look out . . . You were nearly on the pavement . . . There's something else I'd like to ask you, if you won't think it impertinent . . . You're the still-room chef . . . Well, I was wondering what made you take up that profession . . . I mean . . . I feel it isn't a vocation, that one doesn't suddenly say to oneself at fifteen or sixteen: 'I'm going to be a still-room chef . . .'

"Look out . . . If you swerve like that you'll get mown down by a car . . . You were saying? . . ."

Donge explained, in a dejected voice, that he had been a foster child, and that until he was fifteen he had lived on a farm near Vitry-le-François. Then he had gone to work in a café in the town, first as an errand-boy and then as a waiter.

"After doing my military service, I wasn't very fit, and I wanted to live in the South of France . . . I was a waiter in Marseilles and Cannes. Then they decided, at the Miramar, that I didn't look right to wait at table . . . I looked 'awkward,' was the word the manager used . . . I was put in the still-room . . . I was there for years and then I took the job of still-room chef at the Majestic."

They were crossing the Pont de Saint-Cloud. After turning down two or three narrow streets they reached the bottom of a fairly steep incline, and Prosper Donge got off his bike.

"Are you coming any farther?" he asked.

"If you don't mind. After spending a day in the hotel basement, I can appreciate even more your desire to live in the country . . . Do you do any gardening?"

"A little . . ."

"Flowers?"

"Flowers and vegetables . . ."

Now they were going up a badly surfaced, badly lit street, pushing their bicycles; their breath came more quickly, and they didn't talk much.

"Do you know what I discovered while I was nosing about in the basement and talking to everyone I could see? That three people, at least, slept in the hotel basement last night. First, Jean Ramuel . . . It appears . . . it's rather amusing . . . it appears that he has an impossibly difficult mistress and that she periodically shuts him out of the house . . . For the last three or four days she's done it again and he's been sleeping at the Majestic . . . Does the manager know?"

"It's not officially allowed, but he turns a blind eye . . ."

"The professional dancing-partner slept there too . . . the one you call Zebio . . . A strange bloke, isn't he? To look at, he seems too good to be true . . . He's called Eusebio Fualdès on the studio portraits in the grill-room . . . Then, when you read his identity papers you discover that he was born in Lille, in spite of his dark skin, and that his real name is Edgar Fagonet . . . There was a dance, yesterday evening, in honour of a filmstar . . . He was there until half past three in the morning . . . It seems that he's so poor that he decided to sleep at the hotel rather than get a taxi . . ."

Prosper Donge had stopped, near a lamppost, and stood there, his face scarlet, his expression anxious.

"What are you doing?" Maigret asked.

"I'm there . . . I . . ."

Light filtered under the door of a little detached house of millstone grit.

"Would it be a great nuisance if I came in for a moment?"

Maigret could have sworn that the poor great oaf's legs were trembling, that his throat was constricted and that he felt ready to faint. He finally managed to stutter: "If you like . . ."

He opened the door with his key, pushed his bike into the hall, and announced, in what was probably his usual way: "It's me!"

There was a glass door at the end of the passage, leading to the kitchen; the light was on. Donge went in.

"This is . . ."

Charlotte was sitting by the stove, with her feet on the hob, and was sewing a shrimp-pink silk petticoat, lolling in her chair.

She looked embarrassed, took her feet off the stove and tried to find her slippers under the chair.

"Oh! There's someone with you . . . Please excuse me, monsieur . . ."

There was a cup with some dregs of coffee on the table, and a plate with some cake crumbs.

"Come in . . . Sit down . . . Prosper so rarely brings anyone home . . ."

It was hot. The wireless—a smart new one—was on. Charlotte was in her dressing-gown, with her stockings rolled down below the knee.

"A superintendent? What's going on?" she said anxiously, when Donge introduced Maigret.

"Nothing, madame . . . I happened to be working at the Majestic today, and I met your husband there . . ."

At the word husband, she looked at Prosper and burst out laughing.

"Did he tell you we were married?"

"I imagined . . ."

"No, no! . . . Sit down . . . We're just living together . . . I think we're really more like friends than anything else . . . Aren't we, Prosper? . . . We've known each other so long! . . . Mind you, if I wanted him to marry me . . . But as I always say to him, what difference would it make? . . . Everyone who knows me knows I was a dancer, and then a nightclub hostess, on the Riviera . . . And that if I hadn't got so fat, I wouldn't have needed to work in the cloakroom in a club in the Rue Fontaine . . . Oh, Prosper . . . did you remember the payment on the wireless?"

"Yes, it's all done . . ."

An agricultural programme was announced on the radio and Charlotte switched it off, noticed that her dressing-gown was open and pinned it together with a large nappy pin. Some leftovers were heating in a pan on the stove. Charlotte wondered whether to lay the table. And Prosper Donge didn't know what to do or where to go.

"We could go into the sitting-room . . ." he suggested.

"You forget there's no fire there . . . You'll freeze! . . . If you two want to talk, I can go up and get dressed . . . You see, superintendent, we play a sort of game of musical chairs . . . When I get back, he goes out . . . When he gets back it's almost time for me to go, and we just about have time to have something to eat together . . . And even our days off hardly ever seem to coincide, so that when he has a free day he has to get his own lunch . . . Would you like a drink? . . . Can you get him something, Prosper? . . . I'll go up . . ."

Maigret hurriedly interrupted: "Not at all, madame . . . Do please stay . . . I'm just off . . . You see a crime was committed this morning, at the Majestic . . . I wanted to ask your . . . your friend a few questions, as the crime occurred in the basement, at a time when he was almost the only person down there."

He had to make an effort to continue the cruel game, because Donge's face—did he look like a fish, or was it a sheep?—Donge's face expressed so much painful anguish. He was trying to keep calm. He almost succeeded. But at the cost of how much inner turmoil?

Only Charlotte seemed unmoved, and calmly poured out the drinks in small gold-rimmed glasses.

"Something to do with one of the staff?" she said with surprise, but still unperturbed.

"In the basement, but not one of the staff . . . That is what is so puzzling about the whole affair . . . Imagine to yourself a hotel guest, from one of the luxury suites, staying at the Majestic with her husband, her son, a nanny and a governess . . . A suite costing more than a thousand francs a day . . . Well, at six o'clock in the morning she is strangled, not in her room, but in the cloakroom in the basement . . . In all probability, the crime was committed there . . . What was the woman doing in the basement? Who had lured her down there, and why? . . . Especially at a time when people of that sort are usually still fast asleep . . ."

It was barely noticeable: a slight knitting of the brows, as if an idea had occurred to Charlotte and was immediately dismissed. A quick glance at Prosper who was warming his hands over the stove. He had very white hands, with square fingers, covered with red hairs.

But Maigret continued relentlessly: "It won't be easy to find out what this Mrs. Clark had come down to the basement to do . . ."

He held his breath, forced himself to remain motionless, to look as if he were studying the oilcloth tablecloth. You could have heard a pin drop.

Maigret seemed to be trying to give Charlotte time to regain her composure. She had frozen. Her mouth was half open, but no words came out. Then they heard her make a vague noise which sounded like: "Ah!"

Too bad! It was his job. His duty.

"I was wondering if you knew her . . ."

"Me?"

"Not by the name of Mrs. Clark, which she has only been called for a little over six years, but under the name of Émilienne, or rather Mimi . . . She was a hostess, in Cannes, at the time when . . ."

Poor plump Charlotte! What a bad actress she was. Looking at the ceiling like that as if she were racking her memory. Making her eyes look much too rounded and innocent!

"Émilienne? . . . Mimi? . . . No! I don't think . . . You're sure it was Cannes?"

"In a club which was then called La Belle Étoile, just behind the Croisette . . ."

"It's strange . . . I don't remember a Mimi . . . Do you, Prosper?"

It was a miracle he didn't choke. What was the point of forcing him to talk, when his throat was constricted as if by a vice?

"N—no . . ."

Nothing had outwardly changed. There was still that pleasant homely smell in the kitchen, the walls of the little house exuding a reassuring warmth, still the familiar smell of meat braising on a bed of golden onions. The red-and-white-checked oilcloth on the table. Cake crumbs. Like most women who have a tendency to grow fat, Charlotte probably went in for orgies of solitary cake-eating.

And the shrimp-pink silk petticoat!

Then suddenly, the tension evaporated. For no apparent reason. Someone coming in would probably have thought that the Donge family were quietly entertaining a neighbour.

Only none of them dared say a word. Poor Prosper, his skin pitted as a sieve with pock marks, had shut his periwinkle-blue eyes and was standing swaying by the stove, looking as though he would fall on the kitchen floor at any minute.

Maigret got up with a sigh.

"I'm so sorry to have disturbed you . . . It's time I . . ."

"I'll come to the door with you . . ." Charlotte said quickly. "It's time I got dressed anyway . . . I have to be there at ten, and there's only one bus an hour in the evenings . . . So . . ."

"Goodnight, Donge . . ."

"Goo—"

He possibly said the rest, but they didn't hear him. Maigret found his bicycle outside. She shut the door. He nearly looked through the keyhole, but someone was coming down the road and he didn't want to be caught in that position.

He braked all the way down the hill, and stopped in front of a bistro.

"Can you keep this bicycle for me, if I send for it tomorrow morning?"

He swallowed the first thing that came to hand and went to wait for the bus at the Pont de Saint-Cloud. For more than an hour Police Sergeant Lucas had been telephoning frantically, trying in vain to locate his boss.

3

CHARLOTTE AT THE PÉLICAN

"There you are at last, Monsieur Maigret!"

Standing in the doorway of his flat in the Boulevard Richard-Lenoir, the superintendent couldn't help smiling, not because his wife called him "Monsieur Maigret," which she often did when she was joking, but at the warm smell which came to meet him and which reminded him . . .

It was a long way from Saint-Cloud and he lived in a very different milieu from that of the unmarried Donge couple . . . But nevertheless, on his return he found Madame Maigret sewing, not in the kitchen, but in the dining-room, her feet not on the cooker but on the dining-room stove. And he could have sworn that here too there were some cake crumbs tucked away somewhere.

A hanging lamp above the round table. A cloth with a large round soup tureen in the middle, a carafe of wine, a carafe of water, and table-napkins in round silver rings. The smell coming from the kitchen was exactly the same as that from the Donges' stew . . .

"They've rung three times."

"From the House?"

That was what he and his colleagues called Police Headquarters.

He took off his coat with a sigh of relief, warmed his hands over the stove for a minute, and remembered that Prosper Donge had done exactly the same a short while ago. Then he picked up the receiver and dialled a number.

"Is that you, chief?" asked Lucas's kindly voice at the other end of the line. "All right? . . . Anything new? . . . I've got one or two small things to report, which is why I'm still here . . . First, about the governess . . .

"Janvier has been shadowing her since she left the Majestic . . . Do you know what Janvier says about her? . . . He says that in her country she must be a gangster, not a governess . . .

"Hello! . . . Well I'll give you a brief run-down of what happened . . . She left the hotel soon after talking to you . . . Instead of taking the taxi the doorman had called for her, she jumped into a taxi which was passing and Janvier was hard put to it not to lose her . . .

"When they got to the Grands Boulevards, she leapt down the métro . . . then twice doubled back on her tracks. Janvier didn't give up and followed her to the Gare de Lyon . . . He was afraid she might take a train, because he hadn't enough money on him . . .

"The Rome Express was about to leave from Platform 4—in ten minutes' time. Ellen Darroman looked in all the compartments . . . Just as she was turning back, disappointed, a tall, very elegant bloke arrived, carrying a bag . . ."

"Oswald J. Clark . . ." said Maigret, who was looking vaguely at his wife, while listening. "She obviously wanted to warn him . . ."

"According to Janvier, it appears that they met rather as good friends than as an employer and his employee . . . Have you seen Clark? He's a great tall, lanky devil; muscular, with the open, healthy face of a baseball player . . . They went along the platform arguing, as if Clark was still thinking of going . . . When the train started, he still hadn't made up his mind, because it looked for a minute as though he was going to jump into the train.

"Then they went out of the station. They hailed a taxi. A few minutes later, they were at the American Embassy, in the Avenue Gabriel . . .

"They then went to the Avenue Friedland, to see a consulting barrister, a *solicitor* as they call it . . .

"The solicitor telephoned the examining magistrate, and threequarters of an hour later all three of them arrived at the Palais de Justice and were taken at once to the magistrate's office . . .

"I don't know what went on inside, but the magistrate wanted you to telephone him as soon as you got back . . . It seems it is very urgent . . .

"To conclude Janvier's story, after leaving the Palais de Justice, our three characters went to the Forensic Laboratory to identify the body officially . . . Then they went back to the Majestic and there, Clark had two whiskies in the bar with the solicitor while the young woman went up to her room . . .

"That's all, chief . . . The magistrate seems very anxious to have a word with you . . . What time is it? He'll be at home until eight; Turbigo 25–62 . . . Then he's having dinner with some friends, whose number he gave me . . . Just a minute . . . Galvani 47–53 . . .

"Do you need me any more, chief? Goodnight . . . Torrence will be on duty tonight . . ."

"Can I serve the soup?" Madame Maigret asked, sighing, shaking little bits of cotton off her dress.

"Get my dinner-jacket first . . ."

As it was after eight, he dialled Galvani 47–53. It was the number of a young deputy. A maid answered and he could hear the sound of knives and forks and an excited buzz of conversation.

"I'll go and call the magistrate . . . Who is speaking? Superintendent Négret? . . ."

Through the open door of the bedroom, he could see the wardrobe and Madame Maigret taking out his dinner-jacket . . .

"Is that you, superintendent? . . . Hum . . . Ha . . . You don't speak English, do you? . . . Hello! Don't ring off . . . That's what I thought . . . I wanted to say . . . Hum! . . . it's about this case, naturally . . . I think it would be better if you didn't concern yourself with . . . I mean not directly . . . with Mr. Clark and his staff . . ."

A slight smile hovered round Maigret's mouth.

"Monsieur Clark came to see me this afternoon with the governess . . . He's a man of some standing, with important connections . . . Before he came to see me, I had

had a call from the American Embassy who gave me a
very good account of him ... So you see what I mean? ...
In a case like this, one must be careful not to make a
mistake ...

"Monsieur Clark was with his solicitor and insisted on
his statement being taken down ...

"Hello! Are you still there, superintendent?"

"Yes, sir, I'm listening ..."

The sound of forks in the background. The conversation had ceased. No doubt the deputy's guests were listening attentively to what the magistrate was saying.

"I'll put you briefly in the picture ... Tomorrow morning
my clerk can let you have the text of the statement ...
Monsieur Clark did have to go to Rome, then on to various
other capitals, for business reasons ... He had recently become engaged to Miss Ellen Darroman ..."

"Excuse me, sir. You said engaged? I thought Monsieur
Clark was married ..."

"Yes, yes ... That doesn't mean that he didn't intend
getting divorced shortly ... His wife didn't know yet ...
We can therefore say engaged ... He took advantage of
the trip to Rome to ..."

"To spend a night in Paris first with Miss Darroman ..."

"Quite. But you're wrong, superintendent, to indulge
in sarcasm. Clark made an excellent impression on me.
Morals aren't quite the same in his country as in ours, and
divorce over there ... Well, he made no secret of how he
had spent the night ... In your absence, I referred the matter to Inspector Ducuing for verification, to make doubly

sure, but I'm certain Clark wasn't lying . . . Under the circumstances, it would be unfortunate if . . ."

Which meant, in fact:

"We are dealing with a man of the world, who has the protection of the American Embassy. So in the circumstances, don't interfere, because you're likely to be tactless and offend him. See the people in the basement, the maids and so on. But leave Clark to me—I'll deal with him myself!"

"I understand, sir! Of course, sir . . ."

And turning to his wife:

"You can serve the soup, Madame Maigret!"

———

It was nearly midnight. The long corridor at Police Headquarters was deserted, and so dimly lit that it seemed to be filled with a dense smog. Maigret's patent-leather shoes, which he seldom wore, creaked like those of a first-time communicant.

In his office, he began by raking the stove and warming his hands, then, pipe in mouth, he opened the door of the inspectors' office.

Ducuing was there, busy telling Torrence a story which seemed to be amusing them both highly; both men were in great good humour.

"Well, lads?"

And Maigret sat down on a corner of the wooden, ink-stained table, tapping the ash from his pipe on to the floor. He could relax here. The two inspectors had had beer sent

up from the Brasserie Dauphine and the superintendent
was pleased to see they hadn't forgotten him.

"You know, chief, that man Clark's an odd bloke . . . I
went to have a good look at him in the Majestic bar, so that
I could see him at close quarters and register his appearance . . . And at that point I thought he looked the typical
businessman, rather a tough customer in fact . . . Well,
now I know how he spent last night, and I can assure you
he's a bit of a lad . . ."

Torrence couldn't help eyeing the superintendent's
gleaming white shirt-front, adorned with two pearls, which
he didn't often see him wearing.

"Listen . . . First he and the girl dined in a cheap restaurant in the Rue Lepic . . . You know the kind I mean . . .
The proprietor noticed them, because he doesn't often get
asked for real champagne . . . Then they asked where there
was a merry-go-round . . . They had difficulty in explaining
what they wanted . . . He finally directed them to the Foire
du Trône . . .

"I caught up with them again there . . . I don't know
if they had a ride on the merry-go-round, but I imagine
they did . . . They also had a go at the rifle range, I know,
because Clark spent over a hundred francs there, much to
the amazement of the good lady running it . . .

"You know the kind of thing . . . Wandering through
the crowd, arm in arm, like two young lovers . . . But now
we're coming to the best part . . . Listen . . .

"You know Eugène the Muscle Man's booth? At the
end of his show he threw down the gauntlet to the

crowd . . . There was a sort of colossus there who took up the challenge . . . Well . . . our Clark took him on . . . He went to get undressed behind a filthy bit of canvas and made short work of the said colossus . . . I imagine the girl was applauding in the front row of the crowd . . . Everyone was shouting:

"'Go it, the Englishman! . . . Bash his face in!'

"After which our two lovers went dancing at the Moulin de la Galette . . . And at about three they were to be seen at the Coupole, eating grilled sausages, and I imagine they then went quietly off to bye-byes . . .

"The Hotel Aiglon has no doorman. Only a night porter who sleeps in his little room and pulls the door-pull without bothering too much about who comes in . . . He remembers hearing someone talking in English at about four in the morning . . . He says no one went out . . .

"And that's it! Don't you think it's rather an odd evening for people who are supposed to be staying at the Majestic?"

Maigret didn't answer one way or the other, and, glancing at his wristwatch, which he only wore on special occasions (it was a twentieth wedding anniversary present), got up from the table where he'd been sitting.

"Goodnight, children . . ."

He was already at the door, when he came back to finish his glass of beer. He had to walk two or three hundred yards before he found a taxi.

"Rue Fontaine . . ."

It was 1 a.m. Night life in Montmartre was in full swing. A Negro met him at the door of the Pélican and he was obliged to leave his coat and hat in the cloakroom. He hesitated a bit, as if unsure of himself, on entering the main room, where rolls of coloured thread and streamers were flying through the air.

"A table by the cabaret? . . . This way . . . Are you alone?"

He was reduced to muttering under his breath to the maître d'hôtel, who hadn't recognized him: "Idiot!"

The barman, however, had spotted him at once, and was whispering to two hostesses who were propping themselves up at the bar.

Maigret sat down at a table and, as he couldn't drink beer there, ordered a brandy and water. Less than ten minutes later the proprietor, who had been discreetly summoned, came to sit down opposite him.

"Nothing out of order, I hope, superintendent? . . . You know I've always abided by the rules and . . ."

He glanced round the room, as if to see what could have caused this unexpected visit from the police.

"Nothing . . ." Maigret replied. "I felt in need of entertainment . . ."

He pulled his pipe out of his pocket, but saw from the proprietor's face that it would be out of place there, and put it back, sighing.

"If you need any information of any kind . . ." the other said, winking. "But I know all my staff personally . . . I don't think there's anyone here at present who could be of interest to you . . . As for the customers, you can see for yourself . . . The usual crowd . . . Foreigners, people up from the provinces . . . Look! That man over there with Léa is a deputy . . ."

Maigret got up and walked heavily over to the stairs leading to the toilets. These were in a brightly lit basement room, with bluish tiles on the walls. Wooden telephone booths. Mirrors. And a long table on which were numerous toilet articles: brushes, combs, a manicure set, every conceivable shade of powder, rouge and so on . . .

"It's always the same when you dance with him. Give me another pair of stockings, Charlotte . . ."

A plump young woman in an evening dress was sitting on a chair and had already taken off one stocking. She sat there with her skirt hitched up, inspecting her bare foot, while Charlotte rummaged in a drawer.

"Size 44, sheer ones, again?"

"Yes, that will do. I'll take those. If a bloke doesn't know how to dance, he ought at least . . ."

She caught sight of Maigret in the glass and went on putting on her new stockings, glancing at him occasionally as she did so. Charlotte turned round. She, too, saw the superintendent, who saw her turn visibly paler.

"Ah! It's you . . ."

She forced a laugh. She was no longer the same woman who had put her feet on the hob and who stuffed herself with pastries, in the little house in Saint-Cloud.

Her blonde hair was dressed with so much care that the waves seemed permanently glued in place. Her skin was a sugary pink. Her rounded figure was sheathed in a very simple black silk dress, over which she wore a frilly little lace apron of the kind usually only worn by soubrettes in the theatre.

"I'll pay for those with the rest, Charlotte . . ."

"Yes, all right . . ."

The girl realized that the stranger was only waiting for her to go and, as soon as she had her shoes on again, she hurried upstairs.

Charlotte, who was making a show of tidying the brushes and combs, was finally forced to ask: "What do you want?"

Maigret didn't answer. He had sat down on the chair left vacant by the girl with the laddered stockings. As he was in the basement he seized the chance of filling his pipe, slowly, with immense care.

"If you think I know anything, you're mistaken . . ."

It is a strange fact that women who have a placid temperament are the ones who show their emotions the most. Charlotte was trying to keep calm, but she couldn't prevent the waves of colour mounting to her face, or her hands moving so clumsily over the toilet articles that she dropped a nail-polisher.

"I could see, from the way you looked at me, just now, when you visited our house, that you thought . . ."

"I take it you never knew a dancer or nightclub hostess called Mimi, is that correct?"

"No, never!"

"And yet you were a bar girl in Cannes for a long time . . . You were there at the same time as this Mimi . . ."

"There isn't only one nightclub in Cannes, and you don't meet everyone, you know . . ."

"You were at the Belle Étoile, weren't you?"

"What if I was?"

"Nothing . . . I just wanted to come and have a chat with you . . ."

They were silent for at least five minutes, because a customer came down, washed his hands, combed his hair, then asked for a cloth to polish his patent-leather shoes with. When he had finally left a five-franc piece in the saucer, the superintendent continued: "I feel great sympathy for Prosper Donge . . . I feel sure he's the nicest man in the world . . ."

"Oh yes! You don't know how good he is!" she cried fervently.

"He had a miserable childhood and he seems to have always had to struggle for . . ."

"And do you know he didn't pass any exams at school and everything he's learnt he's taught himself? . . . If you look in his still-room you'll find books which people like us don't usually read . . . He's always had a passion for learning things . . . He always dreamt of . . ."

She suddenly stopped, tried to regain her composure.

"Did I hear the telephone ring?"

"No, I don't think so . . ."

"What was I saying?"

"That he always dreamt of . . ."

"Oh well! There's no secret about it. He would have liked to have had a son, make someone of him . . . He chose badly with me, poor lad, because since my operation I can't have children."

"Do you know Jean Ramuel?"

"No. I know he's the bookkeeper and that he's not

very well, that's all. Prosper doesn't tell me much about the Majestic . . . Not like me; I tell him everything that happens here . . ."

Having reassured her, he tried to make a bit of headway again.

"You see, what struck me was . . . I oughtn't to tell you this . . . it's officially a secret . . . But I feel sure it won't go any further . . . Well, the automatic which was found in this Mrs. Clark's handbag had been bought the day before at a gunsmith's in the Faubourg Saint-Honoré . . . Don't you think that that's very odd? There's this rich, married woman, a mother of a family, who arrives from New York and stays in a luxury hotel in the Champs-Élysées, and who suddenly feels the need to buy a gun . . . And note that it wasn't a pretty little lady's pistol, but a proper weapon . . ."

He avoided her eye, looked at the gleaming toecaps of his shoes, as if amazed at his own smartness.

"Now we know that this same woman slipped down a back staircase a few hours later, to get to the hotel basement . . . One is bound to think that she had a rendezvous . . . And to conclude that it was in view of this rendezvous that she had bought her gun. Suppose for a moment that this woman, who is now so respectable, had a stormy past in days gone by and that someone who knew her at that time had tried to blackmail her . . . Do you know if Ramuel ever lived on the Riviera? . . . Or a certain professional dancing-partner called Zebio? . . ."

"I don't know him."

He could tell, without looking at her, that she was on the point of bursting into tears.

"And there's one other person—the night porter—who could have killed her, because he went down to the basement at about six in the morning . . . It was Prosper Donge who heard him going up the back stairs . . . Not to mention any of the room waiters . . . It's a great pity that you didn't know Mimi in Cannes . . . You could have given me details of all the people she knew then . . . Oh well! I would have liked not to have had to go to Cannes . . . I'm bound to be able to find some of the people who knew her, down there . . ."

He got up, tapped out his pipe, felt in his pocket for some change for the saucer.

"You don't need to do that!" she protested.

"Goodnight . . . I wonder what time there's a train . . ."

As soon as he got upstairs, he paid his bill and rushed across the street to the bar opposite, a café frequented by employees from all the nightclubs in the district.

"The telephone, please . . ."

He got on to the exchange.

"Judicial Police, here. Someone from the Pélican will probably ask you for a Cannes number. Don't connect them too quickly . . . Wait till I get to you . . ."

He leapt into a taxi. Rushed to the telephone exchange and made himself known to the night supervisor.

"Give me some headphones . . . Have they asked for Cannes?"

"Yes, a minute ago . . . I found out whose number it

was . . . It's the Brasserie des Artistes, which stays open all night . . . Shall I put them through?"

Maigret put on the headphones and waited. Some of the telephone girls, also wearing headphones, stared at him curiously.

"I'm putting you through to Cannes 18–43, Mademoiselle . . ."

"Thank you . . . Hello! The Brasserie des Artistes? . . . Who's speaking? . . . Is that you, Jean? . . . It's Charlotte here . . . Yes! . . . Charlotte from the Belle Étoile . . . Wait . . . I'll shut the door . . . I think there's someone . . ."

They heard her talking, probably to a customer. Then the sound of a door being shut.

"Listen, Jean dear . . . It's very important . . . I'll write and explain . . . No, I don't think I'd better! It's too risky . . . I'll come and see you later, when it's all over . . . Is Gigi still there? What? Still the same . . . You must be sure to tell her that if anyone questions her about Mimi . . . You remember? . . . Oh no, you weren't there then . . . Well, if she's asked anything at all about her . . . Yes! She knows nothing! . . . And she must be particularly careful not to say anything about Prosper . . ."

"Prosper who?" asked Jean on the other end of the line.

"Never you mind . . . She doesn't know anyone called Prosper, do you hear me? . . . Or Mimi . . . Hello! Are you there . . . Is there someone else on the line? . . ."

Maigret realized that she was scared, that it had perhaps occurred to her that someone was listening to the conversation.

"You understand, Jean dear? . . . I can rely on you? . . . I'm hanging up because there's someone . . ."

Maigret also took off his headphones, and relit his pipe, which had gone out.

"Did you learn what you wanted to know?" asked the supervisor.

"Indeed, yes . . . Get me the Gare de Lyon . . . I must find out what time there's a train for Cannes . . . Provided I've got . . ."

He looked at his dinner-jacket in irritation. Provided he had time to . . .

"Hello! . . . What did you say? . . . Seventeen minutes past four? . . . And I get there at two in the afternoon? . . . Thank you . . ."

Just time to hurry back to the Boulevard Richard-Lenoir and to laugh at Madame Maigret's ill humour.

"Quick, my suit . . . A shirt . . . Socks . . ."

At seventeen minutes past four he was in the Riviera express, sitting opposite a woman who had a horrible pekinese on her lap and who kept looking sideways at Maigret, as though suspecting him of not liking dogs.

At about the same time, Charlotte was getting into a taxi, as she did each night. The driver dealt mostly with customers from the Pélican and took her home free.

At five, Prosper Donge heard a car door slamming, the sound of the engine, footsteps, the key in the door.

But he didn't hear the usual "Pfffttt" of the gas in the kitchen. Without pausing on the ground floor, Charlotte rushed upstairs and banged the door open, panting: "Prosper! . . . Listen! Don't pretend to be asleep . . . The super-intendent . . ."

Before she could explain, she had to undo her bra and take off her girdle, so that her stockings were left dangling round her legs.

"Look, it's serious! Well get up then! . . . Do you think it's easy talking to a man who just lies there! . . ."

4

GIGI AND THE CARNIVAL

For the next three hours, Maigret had the unpleasant feeling that he was floundering in a sort of no man's land between dream and reality. Perhaps it was his fault? Until after Lyons, as far as about Montélimar, the train had rolled through a tunnel of mist. The woman with the little dog, opposite the superintendent, didn't budge from her seat, and there were no empty compartments.

Maigret couldn't get comfortable. It was too hot. If he opened the window, it was too cold. So he had gone along to the restaurant car and, to cheer himself up, had drunk some of everything—coffee, then brandy and then beer.

At about eleven, feeling sick, he told himself he'd feel better if he ate something and ordered some ham and eggs, which were no improvement on the rest.

He was suffering from his sleepless night, the long hours in the train; he was in a very bad temper in fact. After leaving Marseilles, he fell asleep in his corner, with his mouth open, and started awake, stupid with surprise, when he heard Cannes announced.

There was mimosa everywhere, under a brilliant July 14 sun, on the engines, on the carriages, on the station railings.

And crowds of holidaymakers in light clothes, the men in white trousers . . .

Dozens of them were pouring out of a local train, wearing peaked caps, with brass instruments under their arms. He was hardly out of the station before he ran into another band, already rending the air with martial notes.

It was an orgy of light, sound, colour. With flags, banners and oriflammes flying on all sides, and everywhere, the golden yellow mimosa, filling the whole town with its all-pervading, sweetish scent.

"Excuse me, sergeant," he asked a festive-looking policeman, "can you tell me what it's all about?"

The man looked at him as though he had landed from the moon.

"Not heard of the Battle of Flowers?"

Other brass bands were winding through the streets, making for the sea, which could be seen from time to time, lying, pastel blue, at the end of a street.

Later he remembered a little girl dressed as a pierrette, being dragged hurriedly along by her mother, probably in order to get a good place for the pageant. There would have been nothing unusual about it if the little girl hadn't worn a strange mask over her face, with a long nose, red cheeks and drooping Chinese moustache. Trotting along on her chubby little legs . . .

He had no need to ask the way. Going down a quiet street towards the Croisette he saw a sign: BRASSERIE DES ARTISTES. A door farther on: HOTEL. And he saw at a glance what kind of hotel it was.

He went in. Four men dressed in black, with rigid bow ties and white dickeys, were playing *belote*, while waiting to go and take up their positions as croupiers in the casino. By the window, there was a girl eating sauerkraut. The waiter was wiping the tables. A young man, who looked as though he was the proprietor, was reading a newspaper behind the bar. And from outside, from far and near, on all sides, came echoes of the brass bands, and a stale whiff of mimosa, dust kicked up by the feet of the crowd, shouts and the honking of hooters . . .

"A half!" grunted Maigret, at last able to take off his heavy overcoat.

He found it almost embarrassing to be as darkly clad as the croupiers.

He had exchanged glances with the proprietor as soon as he came in.

"Tell me, Monsieur Jean . . ."

And Monsieur Jean was clearly thinking . . .

"That one's probably a cop . . ."

"Have you had this bar a long time?"

"I took it over nearly three years ago . . . Why?"

"And before that?"

"If it's of any interest to you, I was barman at the Café de la Paix, in Monte Carlo . . ."

Barely a hundred metres away, along the Croisette, were the luxury hotels: the Carlton, the Miramar, the Martinez, and others . . .

It was clear that the Brasserie des Artistes was a back-stage prop, as it were, to the more fashionable scene. The

whole street was the same in fact, with dry-cleaning
shops, hairdressers, drivers' bistros, little businesses in the
shadow of the grand hotels.

"The bar's open all night, is it?"

"All night, yes . . ."

Not for the winter visitors, but for the casino and hotel
staff, dancers, hostesses, bellboys, hotel touts, go-betweens
of all kinds, pimps, tipsters, or nightclub bouncers.

"Anything else you want to know?" Monsieur Jean
asked curtly.

"I'd like you to tell me where I can find someone called
Gigi . . ."

"Gigi? . . . Don't know her . . ."

The woman eating sauerkraut was watching them
wearily. The croupiers got up: it was nearly three o'clock.

"Look, Monsieur Jean . . . Have you ever had any
trouble over fruit machines or anything like that? . . ."

"What's that to do with you?"

"I ask because if you've ever been convicted, the case
will be much more serious . . . Charlotte's a good sort . . .
She telephones her friends to ask their help, but forgets
to tell them what it's about . . . So if one has a business
like yours, if one's already been in a spot of trouble once
or twice, one generally doesn't want to become incriminated . . . Well—I'll telephone the vice squad and I'm sure
they won't have any difficulty telling me where I can find
Gigi . . . Have you got a token?"

He had got up, begun walking towards the telephone
booth.

"Excuse me! You spoke of becoming incriminated . . . Is it serious?"

"Well, a murder's involved . . . if a superintendent from the special squad comes down from Paris, you can take it . . ."

"Just a minute, superintendent . . . Do you really want to see Gigi?"

"I've come more than a thousand kilometres to do so . . ."

"Come with me then! But I must warn you that she won't be able to tell you very much . . . Do you know her? . . . She's useless for two days out of three . . . When she's found some dope, I mean, if you get me? . . . Well, yesterday . . ."

"Yesterday, it so happened that, after Charlotte's telephone call, she found some, didn't she? Where is she?"

"This way . . . She's got a room somewhere in town, but last night she was incapable of walking . . ."

A door led to the staircase of the hotel. The proprietor pointed to a room on the landing.

"Someone for you, Gigi!" he shouted.

And he waited at the top of the stairs until Maigret had shut the door. Then went back to his counter, shrugged, and picked up his newspaper, looking a little worried despite himself.

———

The closed curtains let in only a luminous glow. The room was in a mess. A woman lay on the iron bed, with her clothes on, her hair awry, her face buried in the pillow. She began asking in a thick voice: " . . . d'you want?"

Then a very bleary eye appeared.

". . . been here before?"

Pinched nostrils. A wax-like complexion. Gigi was thin, angular, brown as a prune.

". . . time is it? . . . Aren't you going to get undressed? . . ."

She propped herself up on one elbow to drink some water, and stared at Maigret, making a visible effort to pull herself together, and, seeing him sitting gravely on a chair by her bed, asked: "You the doctor? . . ."

"What did Monsieur Jean tell you, last night?"

"Jean? . . . Jean's all right . . . He gave me . . . But what business is it of yours?"

"Yes, I know. He gave you some snow . . . Lie down again . . . And he spoke to you about Mimi and Prosper."

The bands still blaring outside, coming closer and then dying away, and still the stale scent of mimosa, with its own indefinable smell.

"Good old Prosper! . . ."

She spoke as if she were half asleep. Her voice occasionally took on a childish note. Then she suddenly screwed up her eyes and her brow became furrowed as if she were in violent pain. Her mouth was slack.

"You got some, then?"

She wanted some more of the drug. And Maigret had the unpleasant feeling that he was extracting secrets from someone who was sick and delirious.

"You were fond of Prosper, weren't you?"

". . . He's not like other people . . . He's too good . . . He shouldn't have fallen for a woman like Mimi, but that's always the way . . . Do you know him?"

Come on now! Make an effort. Wasn't that what he, Maigret, was there for?

"It was when he was at the Miramar, wasn't it? . . . There were three of you dancing at the Belle Étoile . . . Mimi, Charlotte and you . . ."

She stuttered solemnly: "You mustn't say unkind things about Charlotte . . . She's a good girl . . . And she was in love with Prosper . . . If he'd listened to me . . ."

"I suppose you met at the café, after work . . . Prosper was Mimi's lover . . ."

"He was besotted, he was so much in love with her . . . Poor Prosper! . . . And afterwards, when she . . ."

She sat up suddenly, suspicious: "Is it true that you're a friend of Prosper's?"

"When she had a baby, you mean? . . ."

"Who told you that? I was the only person she wrote to about it . . . But it didn't start like that . . ."

She was listening to the music, which was drawing nearer once more.

"What's that?"

"Nothing . . ."

The flower-decked wagons filing along the Croisette as guns were fired to announce the start. The blazing sun, calm sea, motorboats cutting circles through the water and small yachts gracefully swooping . . .

"Are you sure you haven't got any? . . . You won't go and ask Jean for some? . . ."

"It began when she left with the American?"

"Did Prosper tell you that? . . . Give me another glass of water, there's a good bloke . . . A Yank she met at the Belle

Étoile, who fell in love with her . . . He took her to Deauville, then Biarritz . . . I must admit Mimi knew how to do things properly . . . She wasn't like the rest of us . . . Is Charlotte still working at the Pélican? . . . And look at me! . . ."

She gave a dreadful laugh, disclosing villainous teeth.

"One day, she just wrote that she was going to have a baby and that she was going to make the American think it was his . . . What was he called now? . . . Oswald. Then she wrote again to tell me that it nearly went wrong because the baby had hair the colour of a carrot . . . Can you imagine it! I wouldn't want Prosper to know that . . ."

Was it the effect of the two glasses of water she had drunk? She pulled one leg after the other out of bed, long, thin legs which would attract few male glances. When she was standing upright, she appeared tall, skeleton-like. What long hours she must spend pacing up and down the dark pavements or loitering at a café table before she got any results . . .

Her stare became more fixed. She examined Maigret from head to toe.

"You're from the police, eh?"

She was getting angry. But her mind was still cloudy and she was making an effort to clear her thoughts.

"What did Jean tell me? . . . Ah! . . . And who brought you here anyway? . . . He made me promise not to talk to anyone . . . Admit it! . . . Admit you're from the police . . . And I . . . Why should it matter to the police, if Prosper and Mimi . . ."

The storm broke, suddenly, violently, sickeningly: "You dirty bastard! . . . Swine! . . . You took advantage of me being . . ."

She had opened the door, and the sounds from outside could be heard even more clearly.

"If you don't get out at once, I'll . . . I'll . . ."

It was ridiculous, pathetic. Maigret just managed to sidestep the jug she threw at his legs, and she was still hurling abuse after him as he went down the stairs.

The bar was empty. It was too early still.

"Well?" Monsieur Jean asked, from behind his counter.

Maigret put on his coat and hat, and left a tip for the waiter.

"Did she tell you what you wanted?"

A voice, from the stairs: "Jean! . . . Jean! . . . Come here—I must tell you . . ."

It was poor wretched Gigi, who had padded down in her stockings and now pushed a dishevelled head round the door of the bar.

Maigret thought it better to leave.

On the Croisette, in his black coat and bowler hat, he must have looked like a provincial come to see the carnival on the Côte d'Azur for the first time. Masked figures bumped into him. He had difficulty disentangling himself from the brass bands. On the beach, a few winter visitors ignored the festival and were sunbathing: their near-naked bodies already brown, covered with oil . . .

The Miramar was down there, a vast yellow structure with two or three hundred windows, with its doorman, car

attendants and touts . . . He nearly went in . . . But what
was the use?

Didn't he already know everything he needed to know?
He no longer knew if he was thirsty or drunk. He went into
a bar.

"Have you got a railway timetable?"

"Trains to Paris? There's an express—first, second and
third class—at 20:40 hours . . ."

He drank another half litre. There were hours to fill in.
He couldn't think what to do. And later, he had nightmare
memories of those hours spent in Cannes, amidst the
carnival.

At times, the past became so real to him that he could
literally see Prosper, with his red hair, great candid eyes,
pitted skin, coming out of the Miramar by the little back
door and hurrying across to the Brasserie des Artistes.

The three women, who would be eight years younger
then, would be there having lunch or dinner. Prosper was
ugly. He knew it. And he was passionately in love with
Mimi, the youngest, and prettiest, of the three.

His burning glances must have made them laugh heart-
lessly, at first.

"You shouldn't, Mimi," Charlotte must have intervened. "He's a good sort. You never know how it may turn
out . . ."

Then the Belle Étoile, in the evening. Prosper never set
foot inside. He knew his place. But he met them in the
early morning to eat onion soup at the café . . .

"If a man like that loved me, I would . . ."

Charlotte must have been impressed by his humble devotion. And Gigi wasn't yet on cocaine.

"Don't take any notice, Monsieur Prosper! . . . She pretends to make fun of you, but at heart . . ."

And they had been lovers! Had lived together perhaps. Prosper spent most of his savings on presents. Until the day when a passing American . . .

Had Charlotte told him, later, that the child was definitely his?

Good, kind Charlotte—she knew he didn't love her, that he still loved Mimi, and yet she was living with him, happily, in their little house in Saint-Cloud.

While Gigi slipped farther and farther . . .

"Some flowers, monsieur? . . . To send to your little girlfriend . . ."

The flowerseller spoke ironically, because Maigret didn't look like a man who has a little girlfriend. But he sent a basket of mimosa to Madame Maigret.

Then, as he still had half an hour before the train left, a kind of intuition made him telephone Paris. He was in a little bar near the station. The musicians from the bands now had dusty trousers. Whole carriage-loads of them were leaving for nearby stations, and the fine Sunday afternoon was drawing drowsily to a close.

"Hello! Is that you, chief? . . . You're still in Cannes?"

He could tell from Lucas's voice that he was excited.

"Things have been happening here . . . The examining magistrate is furious . . . He's just telephoned to know what you are doing . . . Hello? They made the discovery only threequarters of an hour ago . . . It was Torrence, who was on duty at the Majestic, who telephoned . . ."

Maigret stood listening to his account in the narrow booth, and grunted from time to time. Through the window, he could see, in the light from the setting sun which filled the bar, the musicians in their white linen trousers and silver-braided caps, and now and then one of them would jokingly sound a long note on his bombardon or trombone, while the golden liquid sparkled in their glasses.

"Right! . . . I'll be there tomorrow morning . . . No! Of course . . . Well if the magistrate insists, you'll have to arrest him . . ."

It had only just happened, then. Downstairs at the Majestic . . . Thé dansant time, with music drifting along the passageways . . . Prosper Donge like a great goldfish in his glass cage . . . Jean Ramuel, yellow as a quince, in his . . .

From what Lucas said—but the inquiry had not yet begun—the night porter had been seen going along the corridors, in his outdoor clothes. No one knew what he was doing there. Everyone had enough to do himself without bothering about what was happening elsewhere.

The night porter was called Justin Colleboeuf. He was a quiet, dull little man, who spent the night alone in the foyer. He didn't read. There was no one to talk to. And he didn't go to sleep. He sat there, on a chair, for hour after hour, staring straight ahead of him.

His wife was the concierge at a new block of flats in Neuilly.

What was Colleboeuf doing there at half past four in the afternoon?

Zebio, the dancer, had gone to the cloakroom to put on his dinner-jacket. Everyone was going about his business. Ramuel had come out of his booth several times.

At five o'clock, Prosper Donge had gone along to the cloakroom. He took off his white jacket and put on his own jacket and coat, and collected his bicycle.

Then a few minutes later a bellboy went into the cloak-room. He noticed that the door of locker 89 was slightly open. The next minute the whole hotel was alerted by his yells.

In the locker, folded over itself, in a grey overcoat, was the body of the night porter. His felt hat was at the back of the cupboard.

Like Mrs. Clark, Justin Colleboeuf had been strangled. The body was still warm.

Meanwhile, Prosper Donge, on his bike, peacefully passed through the Bois de Boulogne, crossed the Pont de Saint-Cloud, and got off his bicycle to go up the steep road to his house.

"A pastis!" Maigret ordered, as there didn't seem to be anything else on the counter.

Then he got into the train, his head as heavy as it had been when he was a child, after a long day in the country, in the blazing sun.

5

SPIT ON THE WINDOW

They had been travelling for some time. Maigret had already taken off his jacket, tie and stiff collar, as the compartment was once again too hot; it was as though hot air, and the smell of the train, was oozing from everywhere—woodwork, floor, seats.

He bent to unlace his shoes. Not content with his free first class pass, he had taken a couchette; too bad if anyone objected. And the guard had promised him that he would have his compartment to himself.

Suddenly, as he was still bending over his shoes, he had the unpleasant feeling that someone was looking at him, from close to. He looked up. There was a pale face peering through the window from the corridor. Dark eyes. A large mouth, badly made up, or rather enlarged, by two streaks of red applied at random, which had then run.

But the most noticeable thing about the face was its expression of dislike, hatred. How had Gigi got there? Before Maigret could put on his shoe again, the girl's face puckered in disgust and she spat on to the window, in his direction, then went back down the corridor.

He remained impassive, and got dressed. Before leaving the compartment, he lit a pipe, as if for moral support. Then he went down the corridor, from carriage to carriage, assiduously looking in each compartment. The train was a long one. Maigret walked through at least ten coaches, bumped into the partitions, had to disturb fifty or more people.

"Sorry . . . Sorry . . ."

He came to where the carpet ended. The third class compartments. People were dozing six to a side. Others were eating. Children stared into space.

In a compartment with two sailors from Toulon who were going "up" to Paris, and an old couple who were nodding off, mouths agape, the woman clutching her basket on her lap, he found Gigi, huddled in a corner.

He hadn't noticed, earlier, in the corridor, how she was dressed. He had been so surprised that he had only taken in that it wasn't the Gigi of the Brasserie des Artistes, with her wandering gaze and slack mouth.

Wrapped in a cheap fur coat, her legs crossed, revealing down-at-heel shoes and a large ladder in her stocking, she stared straight ahead of her. Had she succeeded, on her own, in dragging herself out of the comatose state in which she had been that afternoon? Had someone given her something to take? Or possibly a new dose of cocaine had revived her?

Maigret made no move. He watched her for a while, trying to sign to her; she still took no notice. So he opened the door.

"Would you come out for a minute?"

She hesitated. The two sailors were staring at her. Make a scene? She shrugged and got up to join him, and he shut the door.

"Haven't you had enough?" she hissed at him. "You should be pleased with yourself, shouldn't you! You should feel proud of yourself! You took advantage of the fact that a poor girl was in the state I was in . . ."

He saw that she was about to cry, that her garishly painted mouth was trembling, and turned away.

"And you didn't lose any time in locking him up, did you!"

"Tell me, Gigi. How do you know Prosper has been arrested?"

A weary gesture.

"Haven't you heard? I thought the telephone tapping would see to that . . . It doesn't matter if I tell you, because you'll soon know . . . Charlotte telephoned Jean . . . Prosper had just got back from work when a taxi full of cops arrived and took him away . . . Charlotte's in a terrible state . . . She wanted to know if I'd talked . . . And I did talk, didn't I? I told you enough to . . ."

A violent jolt of the train made her fall against Maigret, and she recoiled in horror.

"I'll be even with you yet! I swear! Even if Prosper did kill that dirty bitch Mimi . . . I'll tell you something, super-intendent . . . On my honour, the honour of a prostitute, a slut who has nothing to lose, I swear to you that if he's condemned to death, I'll find you and plug you full of holes . . ."

She paused for a moment, scornfully. He didn't say anything. He felt it wasn't an empty threat, that she was just the type, in fact, to wait for him on some lonely street corner and empty her automatic into him.

The two sailors were still watching them from the compartment.

"Goodnight," he sighed.

He went back to his compartment, got undressed at last and lay down.

The dimmed light was shedding a vague blue glow on the ceiling. Maigret lay there with his eyes shut, frowning.

One question kept worrying him. Why had the examining magistrate ordered Prosper Donge's arrest? What had the magistrate, who had not left Paris, and who did not know Gigi, or the Brasserie des Artistes, learnt? Why arrest Donge rather than Jean Ramuel or Zebio?

He felt vaguely apprehensive. He knew the magistrate.

He hadn't said anything when he saw him arrive at the Majestic with the public prosecutor, but he had made a face, because he had worked with him in the past.

He was a man of integrity, certainly, a good, family man even, who collected rare editions of books. He had a fine square-cut, grey beard. Maigret had once had to make a raid on a gambling den with him. It was in the daytime, when the place was empty. Pointing to the large baccarat tables shrouded under dust-covers, the magistrate had asked ingenuously: "Are those billiard tables?"

Then, with the same naïveté of a man who has never set foot in a low dive, he had been amazed to discover three exits into three different streets, one of them leading via the basement to another building. He was even more astonished to learn from the account books that certain players were given large advances, because he didn't know that in order to make people play, you have first to get them hooked.

Why had the magistrate, whose name was Bonneau, suddenly decided to have Donge arrested?

Maigret slept badly, waking up each time the train stopped, the noise and jolting of the carriages becoming mixed with his nightmares.

When he got out of his compartment, at the Gare de Lyon, it was still dark and a fine, cold rain was falling. Lucas was there, with his coat collar turned up, stamping his feet to keep himself warm.

"Not too tired, chief?"

"Have you got someone with you?"

"No . . . If you need a police inspector, I saw one of our men in the railway office . . ."

"Go and get him . . ."

Gigi got out, shook hands in a friendly way with the two sailors, and shrugged as she went past the superintendent. She had gone a few steps when she suddenly came back.

"You can have me followed if you want . . . I can tell you in advance that I'm going to see Charlotte . . ."

Lucas came back.

"I couldn't find the inspector . . ."

"Never mind . . . Come on . . ."

They took a taxi.

"Now, let's hear what's happened . . . Why has the magistrate . . ."

"I was going to tell you . . . He summoned me as soon as the second crime had been committed and he had sent some men to arrest Donge . . . He asked me if we had any news, if you'd telephoned and so on . . . Then he handed me a letter, with a nasty smile . . . An anonymous letter . . . I can't remember the exact words . . . It said that Mrs. Clark, who was once a chorus girl called Mimi, had been Donge's mistress, that she had a child by him and that he had often threatened her . . . You look as though you're put out, chief?"

"Go on . . ."

"That's all . . . the magistrate was delighted . . .

"So you see it's a straightforward story!" he concluded. "Common blackmail . . . And as Mrs. Clark no doubt didn't want to pay up . . . I'll go and interrogate Donge shortly in his cell . . ."

"He's there already?"

But the taxi had pulled up at the Quai des Orfèvres. It was half past five in the morning. A thick yellow mist rose from the Seine. Maigret slammed the car door.

"He's at the station? . . . Come with me . . ."

They had to go round the Palais de Justice to get to the Quai de l'Horloge; they went on foot, without hurrying.

"Yes . . . The magistrate telephoned me again at about nine in the evening to say that Donge had refused to speak . . . It appears that he said he would only talk to you . . ."

"Did you get any sleep last night?"

"I got two hours, on a sofa . . ."

"Go and get some rest . . . Be at Headquarters at about midday . . ."

And Maigret went into the Central Police Station. A police van was coming out. There had been a raid at the Bastille and about thirty women had been brought in, some of them new ones without identity cards, and they were sitting round the vast, badly lit room. There was a barrack-room smell, and the air was thick with raucous voices and obscene jokes.

"Where is Donge? . . . Is he asleep?"

"He hasn't slept a wink . . . You'll see for yourself . . ."

The separate boxes were shut by doors with bars, as in a stable. In one of them a man sat, with his head in his hands—a barely discernible figure silhouetted against the darkness.

The key turned in the lock. The hinges creaked. The tall, drooping man got up, as though coming out of a dream. His tie and shoelaces had been taken away. His red hair was unkempt.

"It's you, superintendent . . ." he whispered.

And he rubbed his eyes with his hand, as if to make sure that it was really Maigret who was there.

"I gather you wanted to speak to me?"

"I thought it would be best . . ."

And he asked, with a childish innocence: "The magistrate isn't cross? . . . What could I have told him? . . . He was sure I was guilty . . . He even showed my hands to his clerk, saying they were strangler's hands . . ."

"Come with me . . ."

Maigret hesitated a moment. What was the point of making him wear handcuffs? They must have put them on to bring him to the station. The marks were still on his wrists.

One behind the other, they went along strange corridors, which had little resemblance to those in the Majestic basement. Under the vast Palais de Justice to the Judicial Police building, where they suddenly emerged in a brightly lit passage.

"In here . . . Have you had anything to eat?"

The other indicated that he hadn't. Maigret, who was hungry too, and also thirsty, sent the man on duty to fetch beer and sandwiches.

"Sit down, Donge . . . Gigi is in Paris . . . She must be with Charlotte, by now . . . Cigarette?"

He didn't smoke them, but he always kept cigarettes in his drawer. Prosper clumsily lit one, like someone who has suddenly, in the space of a few hours, lost all his self-assurance. He was troubled by his gaping shoes, the absence of a tie, and the smell which, after only one night in the cells, emanated from his clothes.

Maigret stirred up the fire. All the other offices had central heating, which he loathed, and he had managed to keep the old iron stove which had been there for twenty years.

"Sit down . . . they're bringing us something to eat . . ."

Donge was hesitating as to whether to tell him something, and when he finally decided to speak, stammered in an anguished voice: "Did you see the little boy?"

"No . . ."

"I saw him for a moment in the foyer of the hotel . . . I can swear to you, superintendent, he's . . ."

"Your son. I know."

"You should see him! His hair's as red as mine. He has my hands, my large bones . . . They used to laugh at me, when I was a child, because of my big bones . . ."

The beer and sandwiches arrived. Maigret ate standing up, pacing to and fro across his office, while outside, the sky over Paris began to grow lighter.

"I can't . . ." Donge finally sighed, timidly putting his sandwich back on the plate. "I'm not hungry . . . Whatever happens, they won't take me back at the Majestic now, or anywhere else . . ."

His voice shook. He was waiting for Maigret to help him, but the superintendent let him flounder on.

"Do you think I killed her, as well?"

As Maigret didn't answer, he nodded miserably. He wanted to explain it all now, persuade his interrogator; but he didn't know where to begin.

"You see I never had much to do with women . . . In our trade . . . And always working down in the basement . . . Some of them burst out laughing when I showed I was fond of them . . . With a face like mine, you see . . . Then, when I knew Mimi, at the Brasserie des Artistes . . . There were three of them . . . You know about that . . . And it's odd how it turns out, isn't it? If I had chosen one of the other two . . . But no! I had to fall in love with her! Crazily in love! Superintendent . . . Madly in love! She could have done anything she liked with me! . . . And I thought she'd agree to marry me one day . . . Well, do you know what the magistrate said to me last night? . . . I can't remember what he said, exactly . . . It made me feel ill . . . He said that what I had really been interested in was the money she brought in . . . He took me for a . . ."

Maigret looked out of the window, to spare him further embarrassment, watching the Seine turn palely silver.

"She left with this American . . . I hoped that he'd desert her when he returned to America and that she'd come back to me . . . Then one day we heard that he'd married her . . . The news made me ill . . . It was Charlotte who out of the goodness of her heart, looked after me . . . I told her I couldn't live in Cannes any longer . . . Every street brought back memories . . . I looked for a job in Paris . . . Charlotte offered to come with me. And you may find it hard to believe, but for a long time we lived together as brother and sister . . ."

"Did you know that Mimi had had a child?" Maigret asked, emptying his pipe into the coal bucket.

"I didn't know anything, except that she was living somewhere in America . . . It was only when Charlotte thought I was better . . . In time, you see, we had become a real couple . . . One evening, a neighbour burst into our house; he was beside himself . . . His wife was about to have a baby, much earlier than had been expected . . . He was frantic . . . He asked us to help . . . Charlotte went over . . . The next day, she said to me, 'Poor old Prosper . . . What a state you would have been in, if . . .'

"And then, I don't know quite how it happened . . . bit by bit, she told me that Mimi had a child . . . Mimi had written to Gigi to tell her . . . She had explained that she had used the child as an excuse to make him marry her, although it was definitely mine . . .

"I went to Cannes . . . Gigi showed me the letter, because she'd kept it, but she refused to give it to me and I think she burnt it . . .

"I wrote to America . . . I begged Mimi to give me my son, or at the very least to send me a photograph of him . . . She didn't reply . . . I didn't even know it was the right address . . .

"And I kept thinking: Now my son will be doing this . . . Now he's doing that . . ."

He was silent, choking with emotion, and Maigret pretended to be busy sharpening a pencil, while doors began to bang in the corridors.

"Did Charlotte know you'd written?"

"No. I wrote the letter at the hotel . . . Three years passed . . . One day I was looking at some of the foreign magazines guests leave on their tables . . . I got a shock seeing a photograph of Mimi with a little boy of five . . . It was a newspaper from Detroit, Michigan, and the caption said something like: 'The elegant Mrs. Oswald J. Clark and her son who have just returned from a cruise in the Pacific . . .'

"I wrote again . . ."

"What did you say?" Maigret asked, in an even tone.

"I don't remember. I was going mad. I begged her to reply. I said . . . I think I said I'd go over there, that I'd tell everyone the truth or that if she refused to give me my son, I'd . . ."

"Yes?"

"I swear I wouldn't have done it . . . Yes, I may have threatened to kill her . . . When I think that for a week she was living over my head, with the boy, and that I never suspected . . .

"I only discovered by chance . . . You saw the guests' servants' hall . . . Names don't exist for us, down in the basement . . . We know that Room no. 117 has chocolate in the morning and that no. 452 has eggs and bacon . . . We know the maid from Room no. 123 and the chauffeur from no. 216 . . .

"It was silly . . . I went into the guests' servants' hall . . . I heard a woman speaking English to a chauffeur and she said the name Mrs. Clark . . .

"As I don't speak English, I got the bookkeeper to ask her . . . He asked her if she was talking about a Mrs. Clark from Detroit, and if she had her son with her . . .

"When I learnt they were there, I tried, for a whole day, to catch sight of them, either in the foyer, or in the corridor on their floor . . . But it's difficult for us to go where we want . . . I didn't succeed . . .

"Don't get me wrong . . . I don't know if you'll understand . . . If Mimi had asked to come and live with me again, I couldn't have . . . Don't I love her any more? . . . That may be it . . . I only know that I wouldn't have the heart to leave Charlotte, who's been so kind to me.

"Well, I didn't want to upset things for her . . . I wanted her to find a way to give me back my son . . . I know Charlotte would be only too happy to bring him up . . ."

Maigret looked at him at that moment, and was struck by the intensity of Prosper Donge's emotion. If he hadn't known he had only drunk a half litre—and had not even finished that!—he would have thought he was drunk. The blood had rushed to his face. His eyes shone—great, protruding eyes. He wasn't crying, but he drew great sobbing breaths.

"Have you got any children, sir?"

It was Maigret's turn to turn away, because it was Madame Maigret's great sorrow that she hadn't got children. It was something he tried not to talk about, himself.

"The magistrate talked all the time ... According to him, I had done this and that, for such and such a reason ... But it wasn't like that ... After spending all my free time for the whole day prowling along the corridors of the hotel, in the vain hope of seeing my son ... I didn't know what I was doing any longer ... And the telephone ringing all the time, and the serving-lifts, and my three helpers, and the coffee-pots and milk-jugs to fill ... I sat down in a corner ..."

"In the still-room, you mean?"

"Yes. I wrote a letter ... I wanted to see Mimi ... I remembered that at six o'clock in the morning I was nearly always alone downstairs ... I begged her to come ..."

"You didn't threaten her?"

"Possibly, at the end of the letter ... Yes, I must have written that if she didn't come within three days, I would do what was necessary ..."

"And what did you mean by 'what was necessary'?"

"I don't know . . ."

"Would you have killed her?"

"I couldn't have done it."

"You would have kidnapped the child?"

He gave a pathetic, almost half-witted smile.

"Do you think that would be possible?"

"Would you have told her husband everything?"

Prosper Donge's eyes opened wide in horror.

"No! . . . I swear to you! . . . I think . . . Yes I think that if it had come to the worst, I would have killed her rather than do that, in a moment of anger . . . But that morning, I had a puncture when I got to the Avenue Foch . . . I got to the Majestic nearly quarter of an hour late . . . I didn't see Mimi . . . I thought that she had come and that, as she couldn't find me, she had gone back to her suite . . . If I had known her husband had left, I would have gone up by the back stairs . . . But there again, we in the basement know nothing about what's going on above our heads . . . I was worried . . . That morning, I can't have seemed myself . . ."

Maigret suddenly interrupted him.

"What made you go and open locker 89?"

"I can tell you why . . . And it proves I'm not lying, at any rate to anyone from the police, because if I'd known she was dead, I wouldn't have acted as I did . . . It was about a quarter to nine when the waiter on the second floor sent down the order for no. 203 . . . On the slip there was—you can check it, because the management keep them—there was: one hot chocolate, one egg and bacon and one tea."

"Which meant?"

"I'll explain. I knew that the chocolate was for the boy, the egg and bacon for the nurse . . . So there were only two of them there . . . Every other day at that time there was an order for black coffee and toast for Mimi . . . So, I put the black coffee and toast on the tray too . . . I sent the lift up . . . A few minutes later the coffee and toast were sent back . . . It may seem odd to you to attach so much importance to these details . . . But don't forget that in the basement that's about all we see of what people are doing . . .

"I went to the telephone.

"'Hello! Didn't Mrs. Clark want her breakfast?'

"'Mrs. Clark isn't in her room . . .'

"Please believe me, superintendent . . . The magistrate didn't believe me . . . I was certain that something had happened."

"What did you think had happened?"

"Oh well! . . . I thought of the husband . . . I thought that if he had followed her . . ."

"Who took the letter up for you?"

"A bellboy . . . He assured me he had given it to the right person . . . But those boys lie all the time . . . It comes from being with such an odd lot of people . . . And then Clark could have found the letter . . .

"So—I don't know if anyone saw me, but I opened nearly all the doors in the basement . . . Of course no one takes much notice of anyone else, so perhaps no one noticed me . . . I went into the cloakroom . . ."

"Was the door of locker 89 really open?"

"No. I opened all the empty lockers . . . Do you believe me? . . . Will anyone believe me? . . . No, they won't, will they? . . . And that's why I didn't tell the truth . . . I was waiting . . . I hoped no one would pay any attention to me . . . It was only when I saw that I was the only one you weren't questioning . . . I've never felt so awful as I did that day, while you walked up and down in the basement without saying a single word to me, without seeming to see me! . . . I didn't know what I was doing . . . I forgot the instalment I had to go and pay . . . I came back again . . . Then you joined me in the Bois de Boulogne and I knew you were on my track . . .

"The next morning, Charlotte said when she woke me up: 'Why didn't you tell me you had killed her? . . .'

"So you see, if even Charlotte . . ."

It was broad daylight, and Maigret hadn't noticed. A stream of buses, taxis and delivery vans was going across the bridge. Paris had come to life again.

Then, after a long silence, and in an even more miserable voice, Prosper Donge mumbled: "The boy doesn't even speak French! . . . I asked . . . You couldn't go and see him, superintendent? . . ."

And suddenly frantic: "No! You're not going to let him go away again? . . ."

"Hello! . . . Superintendent Maigret? . . . The boss's asking for you . . ."

Maigret sighed, and went out of his office. It was time to make his report. He was in the head of the Judicial Police's office for twenty minutes.

When he got back, Donge was sitting there unmoving, leaning forwards with his arms crossed on the table and his head on his arms.

The superintendent was worried in spite of himself. But when he touched the prisoner's arm, he slowly looked up, with no attempt to hide his pockmarked face, which was wet with tears.

"The magistrate wants to question you again in his office . . . I advise you to repeat exactly what you have told me . . ."

An inspector was waiting at the door.

"Forgive me if . . ."

Maigret took some handcuffs out of his pocket and there was a double click.

"It's the regulation!" he sighed.

Then, alone in his office once more, he went to open the window and breathed in the damp air. It was a good ten minutes before he went into the inspectors' office.

He appeared fresh and rested again, and asked in his usual way: "All right, children?"

6

CHARLOTTE'S LETTER

There were two policemen sitting on the bench, leaning against the wall, their arms crossed on their chests, and their booted legs stretched out as far as possible, barring the way down the corridor.

A low murmur of voices came through the door beside them. And all along the corridor were other doors flanked by benches, on most of which sat policemen, some with a handcuffed prisoner between them.

It was midday. Maigret was smoking his pipe, waiting to go into examining magistrate Bonneau's office.

"What's that?" he asked one of the policemen, pointing to the door.

The reply was as laconic, and as eloquent, as the question: "Jeweller's in the Rue Saint-Martin . . ."

A girl, sitting slumped on the bench, was staring despairingly at the door of another magistrate. She blew her nose, wiped her eyes, and twisted her hands, tugging at her fingers in a paroxysm of anxiety.

The grim tones of Monsieur Bonneau's voice grew more distinct. The door opened. Maigret automatically stuffed his pipe, which was still warm, into his pocket. The boy who came out, who was at once seized on by the policemen again, had the insolent air of an inveterate ne'er-do-well. He turned back to say to the magistrate with heavy sarcasm: "I'll be happy to come and see you any time, sir!"

He saw Maigret, and frowned; then, as if reassured, winked at the superintendent. The latter's face, at that moment, had the abstracted look of someone who vaguely remembers something without quite knowing what it is.

He heard, from behind the door, which had been left open: "Ask the superintendent to come in . . . You can go now, Monsieur Benoit . . . I won't need you any more this morning . . ."

Maigret went in, still clearly searching his memory. What was it that had struck him about the prisoner who had just left the magistrate's office?

"Good morning, superintendent . . . Not too tired, I hope? . . . Please sit down . . . I don't see your pipe . . . You may smoke . . . Well, how was your trip to Cannes?"

Monsieur Bonneau wasn't a spiteful man, but was obviously delighted to have succeeded where the police had failed. He tried unsuccessfully to hide the gleam of satisfaction which glinted in his eye.

"It's funny that we both learnt the same things, I in Paris, without leaving my office, and you on the Côte d'Azur . . . Don't you think?"

"Very funny, yes . . ."

Maigret had the polite smile of a guest who is forced by his hostess to have a second helping of a dish he detests.

"Well, what are your conclusions on the affair, superintendent? . . . This Prosper Donge? . . . I have his statement here . . . It seems he merely repeated to me what he'd already told you this morning . . . He admits everything, in fact . . ."

"Except the two crimes," Maigret said quietly.

"Except the two crimes, naturally! That would be too good to be true! He admits that he threatened his ex-mistress; he admits that he asked her to meet him at six in the morning in the basement of the hotel, and his letter can't have been very reassuring because the poor woman went straight out to buy a gun . . . Then he tells us this story of his punctured tyre which made him late . . ."

"It isn't a story . . ."

"How do you know? . . . He could have made a puncture in his tyre when he got to the hotel . . ."

"But he didn't . . . I've found the policeman who called out to him about his tyre that morning, at the corner of the Avenue Foch . . ."

"It's only a detail," said the magistrate hurriedly, not wanting to have his beautiful reconstruction undermined. "Tell me, superintendent, have you looked into Donge's past history?"

The glint of satisfaction was now clearly visible in Monsieur Bonneau's eye, and he couldn't help stroking his beard in anticipation.

"I dare say you haven't had time. I made it a point of interest to consult the records . . . I was given his dossier and I discovered that our man, so docile in appearance, is not a first offender . . ."

Maigret was forced to look contrite.

"It's strange," went on the magistrate, "we have these records right above us, on the top floor of the Palais de Justice, and we so often forget to consult them! . . . Well, at the age of sixteen, we find Prosper Donge, who has a job as a washer-up in a café in Vitry-le-François, stealing fifty francs from the till, making off and being caught in a train on his way to Lyons . . . He promises to be good, of course . . . He narrowly escapes being sent to a remand home and is put on probation for two years . . ."

The odd thing was that, while the magistrate was saying all this, Maigret kept thinking: "Where the devil did I see that . . . ?"

And he wasn't thinking of Donge, but of the boy who had come out as he went in.

"Fifteen years later, in Cannes, three months' suspended sentence for criminal assault, and insulting behaviour to a policeman . . . And now, superintendent, perhaps it's time I showed you something . . ."

At which he held out a bit of squared paper like that sold in small shops or used as bill chits in small cafés. The text was written in violet ink, with a spluttery pen, and the writing was that of an ill-educated woman.

It was the famous anonymous letter which had been sent to the magistrate, informing him about Prosper and Mimi's affair.

"Here is the envelope . . . As you see, it was posted between midnight and six in the morning in the postbox in the Place Clichy . . . Place Clichy, you note . . . Now, take a look at this exercise book . . ."

A rather grubby school exercise book, covered with grease marks. It contained cooking recipes—some cut from newspapers and stuck in, others copied out.

This time, Maigret frowned, and the magistrate couldn't disguise a triumphant smile.

"You would agree that it's the same writing? . . . I felt sure you would . . . Well, superintendent, this exercise book was taken from the dresser in a kitchen which you already know, in Saint-Cloud—at Prosper Donge's house, in fact— and these recipes were copied out by a certain Charlotte . . ."

He was so pleased with himself that he made a show of apologizing.

"I know the police and ourselves don't always see things in quite the same light . . . At the Quai des Orfèvres, you have a certain sympathy for a particular kind of person, for certain irregular situations, which we as magistrates have difficulty in sharing . . . Admit, superintendent, it is not always we who are wrong . . . And tell me why, if this Prosper is the upright man he appears, his own mistress, this Charlotte who also pretends to be such a good sort, should send me an anonymous letter to destroy him?"

"I don't know . . ."

Maigret seemed completely bowled over.

"This case can be tidied up quite quickly now. I've sent Donge to the Santé prison. When you've interrogated the woman, Charlotte . . . As for the second crime, it can easily be explained . . . The poor night porter . . . Colleboeuf, I believe? . . . must have been party to the first crime . . . At any rate he knew who the murderer of Mrs. Clark was . . .

He couldn't rest all day . . . And finally no doubt, tortured by indecision, he came back to the Majestic to warn the murderer that he was going to denounce him . . ."

The telephone rang.

"Hello! Yes . . . I'll come at once . . ."

And to Maigret: "It's my wife, to remind me that we have some friends coming to luncheon . . . I will leave you to your inquiry, superintendent . . . I think you now have enough leads to go on . . ."

Maigret was almost at the door, when he came back, with the look of someone who has at last pinned down what he had been trying to remember for some time.

"About Fred, sir . . . It *was* Fred-the-Marseillais you were interrogating when I arrived, wasn't it?"

"It's the sixth time I've interrogated him without discovering the names of his accomplices . . ."

"I met Fred about three weeks ago, at Angelino's in the Place d'Italie . . ."

The magistrate stared at him, clearly unable to see the relevance of this remark.

"Angelino, who has a 'club' frequented by rather dubious types, has been going with the sister of Harry-the-Squint for a year . . ."

The magistrate still didn't understand. And Maigret said modestly, effacing himself as much as his massive frame would allow: "Harry-the-Squint has had three sentences for house-breaking . . . He's an ex-bricklayer whose speciality is tunnelling through walls . . ."

And, with his hand on the door: "Didn't the burglars in

the Rue Saint-Martin get in by the basement by tunnelling through two walls? . . . Goodbye, sir . . ."

He was in a bad mood, all the same. That letter from Charlotte . . . And looking at him, you would have sworn that it wasn't only anger, but that he was also a little sad.

———

He could have sent an inspector. But would an inspector have been able to get the feel of the house as well as he could?

A large, new, luxury building, painted white and with a wrought-iron gateway, in the Avenue de Madrid, by the Bois de Boulogne. The concierge's lodge to the right of the hall, with a glass door, furnished like a proper reception room. Three or four women dozing on chairs. Visiting cards on a tray. Another woman, whose eyes were red, who opened the door and asked: "What do you want?"

The door of a further room was open and there was a corpse lying on the bed, hands folded, a rosary clasped in the fingers, with two candles fluttering in the dim light and box-wood in a bowl of holy water.

They spoke in low tones. Blew their noses. Walked on tiptoe. Maigret made the sign of the cross, sprinkled a little holy water over the body, and stood there for a minute silently contemplating the dead man's nose, which the candle threw into strange relief.

"It's terrible, superintendent . . . Such a good man, without an enemy in the world!"

Above the bed, in an oval frame, a large photograph of

Justin Colleboeuf, in his sergeant-major's uniform, taken at the time when he still had a large moustache. A croix de guerre with three palms and the military medal were fixed to the frame.

"He was in the regular army, superintendent . . . When he got to retiring age, he didn't know what to do to keep himself occupied and insisted on doing work of some kind . . . He was nightwatchman at a club in the Boulevard Haussmann for a while . . . Then someone suggested the job of night porter at the Majestic to him, and he took that . . . You see he was someone who needed very little sleep . . . At the barracks he used to get up nearly every night to go the rounds . . ."

Her neighbours, or possibly relations, nodded sympathetically.

"What did he do in the daytime?" Maigret asked.

"He got back at quarter past seven in the morning, just in time to put out the dustbins for me, because he didn't let me do any of the heavy work . . . Then he stood in the doorway and had a pipe while he waited for the postman, and had a little chat with him . . . The postman had been in the same regiment as my husband, you see . . . Then he went to bed till midday . . . That was all the sleep he needed . . . When he'd had lunch, he walked across the Bois de Boulogne to the Champs-Élysées . . . Sometimes he went into the Majestic to say hello to his colleague on duty here during the day . . . Then he had his usual in the little bar in the Rue de Ponthieu and got back at six o'clock, and left again at seven to go on duty at the hotel . . . He was so regular in his habits that people round here could set their clocks by the time when they saw him go by . . ."

"Is it a long time since he gave up wearing a moustache?"

"He shaved it off when he left the army . . . I thought he looked very funny without it . . . it made him seem less important . . . He even looked smaller somehow . . ."

Maigret inclined his head once more in the direction of the dead man and crept away on tiptoe.

He wasn't far from Saint-Cloud. He was impatient to get there and yet at the same time, for some unknown reason, he was stalling for time. A taxi went past. Oh well! He held up his arm . . .

"To Saint-Cloud . . . I'll explain where . . ."

It was drizzling. The sky was grey. It was only three o'clock but it might have been evening. The houses, in their bare little gardens, with their leafless winter trees, looked desolate.

He rang the bell. It wasn't Charlotte but Gigi who came to the door, while Donge's mistress peered from the kitchen to see who was there.

Still glowering balefully at him, Gigi let him in without saying a word. It was only two days since Maigret had last been there and yet it seemed to him that the house looked different. Perhaps Gigi had brought some of her own chaos with her. The unwashed lunch things were still on the kitchen table.

Gigi was wearing one of Charlotte's dressing-gowns, which was much too big for her, over her nightdress, and an old pair of Prosper's shoes on her bare feet. She was smoking a cigarette, and squinting through the smoke.

Charlotte, who had got up as he went in, was at a loss for words. She hadn't washed. Her skin looked blotchy, and without a bra, her bosom sagged.

He wondered who would speak first. They were giving each other anxious, suspicious looks. Maigret sat down, unabashed, with his bowler on his knee.

"I had a long talk with Prosper this morning," he said at last.

"What did he say?" Charlotte hurriedly asked.

"That he didn't kill Mimi, or the night porter . . ."

"Ah!" Gigi cried triumphantly. "What did I tell you!"

Charlotte couldn't take it in. She seemed at a loss. She wasn't made for drama and seemed perpetually to be looking for something to cling to.

"I also saw the magistrate. He has been sent an anonymous letter concerning Prosper and Mimi . . ."

No reaction. Charlotte was still staring at him with curiosity, her lids heavy, her body limp.

"An anonymous letter?"

He handed her the recipe book which he had brought with him.

"It's your writing in this book, isn't it?"

"Yes . . . Why?"

"Would you be good enough to take a pen? . . . preferably an old one which splutters . . . And paper . . . and ink . . ."

There was a bottle of ink and a penholder on the dresser. Gigi looked from Maigret to her friend in turn, as if ready to intervene the moment she sensed danger.

"Make yourself comfortable . . . And write . . ."

"What shall I write?"

"Don't write anything, Charlotte! You can't trust them . . ."

"Write—There's no danger, I promise you—'*Sir, I am taking the liberty of writing to you about the Donge affair, which I read about in the newspaper . . .*'"

"Why do you spell newspaper with a 'u'?"

"I don't know . . . What should I put?"

On the anonymous letter which he had in his hand, there was a "z."

". . . '*The American woman isn't really an American woman; she was a dancer and her name was Mimi . . .*'"

Maigret shrugged impatiently.

"That will do," he said. "Now, take a look . . ."

The writing was exactly the same. Only the spelling mistakes were different.

"Who wrote that?"

"That's exactly what I would like to know . . ."

"You thought it was me?"

She was choking with anger, and the superintendent hurriedly tried to calm her.

"I didn't think anything . . . What I came to ask you is who, besides you and Gigi, knew about Prosper and Mimi's affair, and particularly about the child? . . ."

"Can you think of anyone, Gigi?"

They thought for a long time, indolently. They seemed to be aimlessly drifting in the untidy house, which had suddenly taken on a sordid aspect. Gigi's nostrils quivered from time to time, and Maigret realized that it wouldn't be long before she was out searching frantically for a fix.

"No . . . Except us three . . ."

"Who was it who got Mimi's letter at the time?"

"It was me," said Gigi, " . . . and before I left Cannes, I found it in a box where I kept some souvenirs . . . I brought it with me . . ."

"Let me see . . ."

"Provided you promise . . ."

"Of course, you fool! Can't you see I'm trying to get Prosper out of the mess."

He felt concerned, irritable. He had begun to have a vague feeling that there were mysterious complications to the affair, but he had not the slightest clue to tell him what they might be.

"Will you promise to give it back?"

He shrugged again, and read:

My dear old Gigi,

Phew! I've made it! I've made it at last! You and Charlotte laughed when I told you I'd get out of there one day and that I'd be a real lady.

Well, ducky, I've done it . . . Oswald and I were married yesterday, and it was a funny kind of wedding, because he wanted it to be in England, where it's quite different from in France. In fact I sometimes wonder at times if I'm really married.

Let Charlotte know. We'll be sailing for America

in three or four days' time. We don't know exactly
when we'll be sailing, because of the strike.

As for poor Prosper, I think it would be best not
to tell him anything. He's a nice boy, but a bit
simple. I don't know how I managed to stay with
him for nearly a year. It must have been my year
for being kind . . .

But still, he's done me a good turn, without
knowing it. Keep this to yourself. No point in
telling Charlotte—she's a great sentimental fool.

I've known for some time that I was pregnant.
You can imagine the face I made when I knew. I
rushed to see a specialist before telling Oswald . . .
We did some calculations . . . Well, it's quite definite
that the baby can't be Oswald's . . . So it's poor
Prosper who . . . Don't ever let him know! He might
get a rush of paternal feeling!

It would take too long to tell you everything . . .
The doctor has been very decent about it . . . By
cheating a bit as to the date of birth (we'll have
to pretend it's a premature delivery), we've
succeeded in convincing Oswald that he's going to
be a father.

He took it very well. Contrary to what one
might think when one first meets him, he's not at
all cold. In fact when we're by ourselves he's like a
child, and the other day, when we were in Paris, we
visited all the pleasure gardens and rode on the
roundabouts . . .

Well, I'm now Mrs. Oswald J. Clark of Detroit (Michigan), and from now on I shall speak English all the time, because Oswald, if you remember, doesn't know a word of French.

I think of you two sometimes. Is Charlotte still just as worried about getting fat? Does she still knit all the time? I bet she'll finish up behind the counter in a haberdasher's shop in the provinces!

As for you, my old Gigi, I don't think you'll ever grow respectable. As the client in the white gaiters said so comically—you remember, the one who gulped down a whole bottle of champagne in one go?—you've got vice in the blood!

Say hello to the Croisette for me and don't burst out laughing when you look at Prosper and imagine him being a father without knowing it.

I'll send you some postcards.

Love and kisses,

Mimi.

"May I take this letter with me?"

It was Charlotte who intervened.

"Let him, Gigi . . . It can't make it any worse . . ."

And as she showed the superintendent out: "Look! . . . Couldn't I get permission to go and see him? He has the right to have his meals sent in from outside, hasn't he? . . . Could you . . ."

And she blushed and held out a thousand franc note to him.

"If he could have a few books too . . . He used to spend all his free time reading . . ."

Rain. A taxi. The streetlamps coming alight. The Bois de Boulogne which Maigret had crossed on his bike, side by side with Donge.

"Put me down by the Majestic, will you?"

The porter followed him a little anxiously as he crossed the foyer without speaking, and took Maigret's coat and hat in the cloakroom. The manager had also seen him, through the crack in his curtains. Everyone knew Maigret—followed him with their eyes.

The bar? Why not? He was thirsty. But he was attracted by a muffled sound of music. Somewhere in the basement a band was softly playing a tango. He went down a staircase carpeted with thick carpet, into a bluish haze. People were eating cakes at little tables. Others were dancing. A waiter came up to the superintendent.

"Bring me a half, please . . ."

"We don't . . ."

Maigret gave him a look and he hurriedly scribbled something on a chit . . . The bills which . . . Maigret watched where it went . . . At the back of the room, to the right of the band, there was a sort of hatch in the wall . . .

On the other side were the glass cages, the still-room, the kitchens, the sculleries, the guests' servants' hall, and, right at the end, near the clocking-on machine, the cloakroom with its hundred metal lockers.

Someone was watching him—he could feel it—and he noticed Zebio dancing with a middle-aged woman covered in jewels.

Was it an illusion? It seemed to Maigret that Zebio's look was trying to tell him something. He turned and saw with a shock that Oswald J. Clark was dancing with his son's governess, Ellen Darroman.

They both seemed utterly oblivious of their surroundings. They were caught up in the ecstasy of new-found love. Solemn, hardly smiling, they were alone on the dance-floor, alone in the world, and when the music stopped they stood there without moving for a minute before going back to their table.

Maigret then noticed that Clark was wearing a thin band of black material on the lapel of his jacket—his way of wearing mourning.

The superintendent's fist tightened on Mimi's letter to Gigi which was in his pocket. He had a terrible desire to . . .

But hadn't the magistrate told him not to get involved with Clark, who was no doubt too much of a gentleman to grapple with a policeman?

The tango was followed by a slow foxtrot. A frothy half followed the route the waiter's order had taken previously—in the opposite direction. The pair were dancing again.

Maigret suddenly got up, forgot to pay for his drink, and hurried to the foyer.

"Is there anyone in Suite 203?" he asked the porter.

"I think the nanny and the boy are up there . . . But . . . If you'd like to wait while I telephone . . ."

"No, please don't do that . . ."

"There's the lift, on your left, sir."

Too late. Maigret had made for the marble staircase and was slowly starting up the stairs, grunting as he went.

7

"WHAT'S HE ON ABOUT?"

Maigret was assailed for a moment by a strange thought, which however he soon forgot. He had reached the second floor of the Majestic and stopped for a moment to get his breath back. On his way up he had met a waiter with a tray, and a bellboy running up the stairs with a bundle of foreign newspapers under his arm.

On this floor there were smartly dressed women getting into the lift, who were probably going down to the thé dansant. They left a trail of scent behind them.

"They are all in their proper places," he thought to himself. "Some behind the scenes and the others in the lounges and foyer . . . The guests on one side and the staff on the other . . ."

But that wasn't what was bothering him, was it? Everyone, round him, was in his allotted place, doing the right thing. It was normal, for instance, for a rich foreign woman to have tea, smoke cigarettes and go out for fittings. It was natural for a waiter to carry a tray, a chambermaid to make beds, a liftman to operate a lift . . .

In short, their functions, such as they were, were clearly defined, settled once and for all.

But if anyone had asked Maigret what he was doing there, what would he have answered?

"I am trying to get a man sent to prison, or even executed . . ."

It was nothing. A slight dizziness, probably caused by the over-luxurious, almost aggressively luxurious setting, and the atmosphere in the tea-room . . .

209 . . . 207 . . . 205 . . . 203 . . . Maigret hesitated for a moment and then knocked. His ear to the door, he could hear a child's voice saying a few words in English, then a woman's voice sounding more distant, and, he imagined, telling him to come in.

He crossed a little hall and found himself in a sitting-room with three windows overlooking the Champs-Élysées. By one of the windows an elderly woman, dressed in a white apron like a nurse, was sitting sewing. It was the nanny, Gertrud Borms, made to look even more severe by the glasses she wore.

But the superintendent paid no attention to her. He was looking at a boy of about six, dressed in plus-fours and a sweater which fitted snugly round his thin frame. The boy was sitting on the carpet, his few toys round him, including a large toy boat, and cars which were exact replicas of various real makes. There was a picture book on his knee which he was looking at when Maigret went in, and after glancing briefly at the visitor, he bent over it again.

When he recounted the scene to Madame Maigret, the superintendent's description went something like this: "She said something like, 'You we you we we well . . .'

"And to gain time, I said very quickly: 'I hope that I'm correct in thinking this is Monsieur Oswald J. Clark's suite? . . .'

"She went on again: 'You we you we we well,' or something of the sort.

"And meanwhile, I was able to get a good look at the boy. A very big head for his age, covered, as I had been told, with hair of a fiery red. The same blue eyes as Prosper Donge—the colour of periwinkles or of certain summer skies . . . A thin neck . . .

"He started talking to his nanny, in English, too, looking at me as he did so, and to me it still sounded like: 'You we you we we well . . .'

"They were evidently asking themselves what I wanted and why I was standing there in the middle of the room. I didn't know myself why I was there. There were flowers worth several hundred francs in a Chinese vase . . .

"The nanny finally got up. She put her work down on the chair, picked up a telephone and spoke to someone.

"'Don't you understand any French, little one?' I asked the child.

"He merely gazed at me with eyes full of suspicion. A few seconds later, an employee in a tailcoat came into the suite. The nanny spoke to him. He then turned to me.

"'She wants to know what you want?'

"'I wanted to see Monsieur Clark . . .'

"'He isn't here . . . She says he is probably down-stairs . . .'

"'Thank you very much . . .'"

And that was that! Maigret had wanted to see Teddy Clark and he had seen him. He went back downstairs thinking about Prosper Donge, shut in his cell at the Santé. Automatically, without thinking, he went on down to the tea-room and, as his beer had not yet been cleared away, he sat down again.

He was in a state of mind he knew well. It was rather as if he were in a daze, although he was conscious of what was happening round him, without attaching any importance to it, without making any effort to place people or things in time or space.

Thus he saw a page go up to Ellen Darroman and say a few words to her. She got up and went to a telephone booth, in which she only remained for a few seconds.

When she came out, she immediately looked round for Maigret. Then she rejoined Clark and said something to him in a low voice, still looking at the superintendent.

In that instant, Maigret had a sudden very definite feeling that something disagreeable was about to happen. He knew that the best thing to do would be to leave at once, but he didn't go.

He would have found it hard to explain why he stayed there, if called on to do so.

It wasn't because he felt it was his professional duty.

There was no need to stay at the thé dansant any longer—
he was out of his element there.

That was precisely it—but he couldn't have put it into
words.

The magistrate had arrested Prosper Donge without
consulting him, hadn't he? And moreover he had forbid-
den him to concern himself with the American?

That was tantamount to saying: "That is not your
world . . . You don't understand it . . . Leave it to me . . ."

And Maigret, plebeian to the core, to the very marrow of
his bones, felt hostile towards the world which surrounded
him here.

Too bad. He would stay all the same. He saw Clark
looking at him in turn, then Clark frowned, and, no doubt
telling his companion to stay where she was, got up. A
dance had just begun. The blue lighting gave way to pink.
The American made his way between the couples and
came and stood in front of the superintendent.

To Maigret, who couldn't understand a word of English,
it still sounded like: "Well you well we we well . . ."

But this time the tone was aggressive and it was clear
that Clark was having difficulty controlling himself.

"What are you saying?"

And Clark burst out even more angrily.

———

That evening, Madame Maigret said, shaking her head:
"Admit it! You did it on purpose! I know that way you
have of looking at people! You'd make an angel lose his
temper . . ."

He didn't admit anything, but there was a twinkle in his eye. Well, what *had* he done anyway? He had stood there in front of the Yankee, with his hands in his jacket pockets, staring at him as if he found the spectacle curious.

Was it his fault? Donge was still uppermost in his mind—Donge who was in prison, not dancing with the very pretty Miss Ellen. No doubt sensing that a drama was about to unfold, she had got up to join them. But before she reached them, Clark had hit out furiously at Maigret's face, with the clean clockwork precision one sees in American films.

Two women having tea at the next table got up screaming. Some of the couples stopped dancing.

Clark seemed to be satisfied. He probably thought that the matter was now settled and that there was nothing further to add.

Maigret didn't even deign to run his hand over his chin. The impact of Clark's fist on his jaw had been clearly audible, but the superintendent's face remained as impassive as if he had been lightly tapped on the head.

Although he hadn't planned it that way, he was delighted at what had happened, and couldn't help smiling when he thought of the examining magistrate's face.

"Gentlemen! . . . Gentlemen! . . ."

Just as it seemed that Maigret would launch himself at his adversary and that the fight would continue, a waiter intervened. Ellen and one of the men who had been dancing grabbed hold of Clark on either side and tried to restrain him, while he still went on talking.

"What's he on about?" Maigret grumbled calmly.

"It doesn't matter! . . . Gentlemen, will you please kindly . . ."

Clark went on talking.

"What's he saying?"

Then, to everyone's surprise, Maigret began negligently to play with a shiny object which he had taken from his pocket and the fashionable women stared in amazement at the handcuffs, which they had so often heard about but never actually seen.

"Waiter, would you be good enough to translate for me? . . . Tell this gentleman that I am obliged to arrest him for insulting an officer of the law while in the course of his duty . . . And tell him too that if he is not prepared to follow me quietly, I shall have regretfully to use these handcuffs . . ."

Clark didn't flinch. He didn't say another word and pushed Ellen, who was clinging to his arm and trying to follow him, aside. Without waiting for his hat or coat he followed closely on the superintendent's heels, and as they crossed the foyer, followed by a small crowd of onlookers, the manager saw them from his office, and raised his hands to heaven in horror.

"Taxi! . . . To the Palais de Justice . . ."

It was dark now. They went up the stairs, along corridors, and stopped outside Monsieur Bonneau's door. Maigret then adopted a humble and contrite attitude which Madame Maigret knew well and which infuriated her.

"I am so sorry, sir . . . I have been obliged, much to my regret, to put Mr. Clark, who you see here, under arrest . . ."

The magistrate had no idea what had happened. He imagined that Maigret suspected the American of having murdered his wife and the night porter.

"Excuse me! Excuse me! On what grounds have you . . ."

It was Clark who answered and to Maigret the words still sounded like a senseless jingle.

"What's he saying?"

The poor magistrate raised his eyebrows and frowned. His own knowledge of English was far from good and he had difficulty himself in following what the American was saying. He mumbled something, and sent his clerk to fetch another clerk who sometimes acted as interpreter.

"What's he on about?" Maigret muttered from time to time.

And Clark, irritated beyond measure by this, burst out, clenching his fists and imitating the superintendent: "What's he saying? . . . What's he saying? . . ."

There had followed another tirade in English.

The interpreter sidled into the room. He was a little bald man, disarmingly humble and timid.

"He says he's an American citizen and that it's intolerable that policemen . . ."

Judging by his tone of voice, Clark had little respect for the police . . .

". . . that policemen should be allowed to follow him about everywhere . . . He says an inspector has been constantly at his heels . . ."

"Is that true, superintendent?"

"He is probably right, sir."

". . . He says another policeman was following Miss Ellen . . ."

"It's very likely . . ."

". . . And you burst into his hotel suite, in his absence . . ."

"I knocked politely on the door and asked the good lady who was there in the politest way in the world if I could see Monsieur Clark . . . After which I went down to the thé dansant to have a glass of beer . . . It was then that this gentleman saw fit to shove his fist in my face . . ."

Monsieur Bonneau was in despair. As if the affair wasn't complicated enough anyway! They had managed to keep the press out of it until now, but after the fracas in the tea-room there would be journalists besieging the Palais de Justice and Police Headquarters on all sides . . .

"I cannot understand, superintendent, why a man like you, with twenty-five years' experience . . ."

And then he nearly lost his temper, because instead of listening to him, Maigret was playing with a bit of paper which he'd taken out of his pocket. It was a letter, written on bluish paper.

"Monsieur Clark certainly went too far. Equally, it is true to say that for your part you omitted to show the tact one would have expected of you in circumstances which . . ."

It had worked. Maigret had to turn away to hide his satisfaction. Clark had become hypnotized by the piece of paper and finally walked up to him and held out his hand.

"Please—"

Maigret appeared surprised, and gave the American

the piece of paper he was holding. The magistrate under-stood less and less, and suspected, not without reason, that the superintendent was up to something.

Then Clark went up to the interpreter and showed him the letter, gabbling away as he did so.

"What's he saying?"

"He says he recognizes his wife's handwriting and wants to know how you came to be in possession of a letter from her . . ."

"Please explain, Monsieur Maigret," Monsieur Bonneau said coldly.

"I beg your pardon, sir . . . It's a document I've just been given . . . I wanted to show it to you, and add it to the dossier . . . Unfortunately Monsieur Clark took it before . . ."

Clark was still talking to the interpreter.

"What's he saying?" said the magistrate, catching the disease.

"He wants me to translate the letter . . . He says if someone has rifled through his wife's things, he will lodge a complaint with his embassy and that . . ."

"Translate . . ."

Maigret, his nerves taut, started filling his pipe, and went over to the window, where he could see the gas lights shining like stars through their misty haloes.

The poor interpreter, his bald pate covered in sweat, translated Mimi's letter to her friend Gigi word by word, wondering as he did so if he dared continue, so horrified was he. The magistrate had drawn closer to read over his shoulder, but Clark, more peremptory than ever, had motioned him aside, saying: "Please—"

He had the air of one guarding his property, as though he wanted to prevent anyone from taking the letter, or from trying to destroy it, or from missing out anything in the translation. He pointed to each word with his finger, demanding the exact meaning.

Monsieur Bonneau, in total despair, went over to join the superintendent, who was smoking his pipe with seeming indifference.

"Did you do this on purpose, superintendent?"

"How could I foresee that Monsieur Clark would thrust his fist in my face?"

"This letter explains everything!"

"With perfect cynicism!"

Good grief! The magistrate had sent Prosper Donge to prison without any proof that he was guilty. And he was perfectly prepared to send Charlotte, Gigi or any of the rest of them to join him!

The interpreter and Clark stood leaning over the table, where the green-shaded lamp shed its circle of light.

Finally Clark stood up. He banged his fist on the table, muttering something which sounded like: "Damned!"

Then he reacted very differently to what one might have expected. He remained calm, and didn't look at any of them. His face had set, and he stared into space. After remaining like that for a long time, during which the poor interpreter looked as though he was trying to gather his courage to apologize to him, he turned round, saw a chair in a corner of the room, and went and sat down, so calmly and simply, that his very simplicity seemed almost tragic.

Maigret, who had been watching him from a distance, could see beads of sweat literally breaking out on the skin above his upper lip.

And Clark, at this moment, was a bit like a boxer who has just received a knock-out blow but who is kept upright by the force of inertia and instinctively looks for some support before going down for good.

There was complete silence in the magistrate's office and they could hear the sound of a typewriter in a neighbouring room.

Clark still made no move. He sat in his corner with his elbows on his knee, his chin in his hands, staring at his feet in their square-toed shoes.

A long time later, they heard him muttering: "Well! . . . Well! . . ."

And Maigret quietly asking the interpreter: "What's he saying?"

The magistrate took the line of pretending to look at his papers. The smoke from Maigret's pipe rose slowly in the air, seeming to drift towards the circle of light round the lamp.

"Well . . ."

Clark's thoughts were far away. God knew where. He finally looked up, and they wondered what he would do next. He took a heavy gold cigarette case out of his pocket, opened it, took out a cigarette and snapped the case shut again. Then, turning to the interpreter, he said: "Please . . ."

He wanted a match. The interpreter didn't smoke. The superintendent handed him a box of matches, and as he took it, Clark glanced at him and gave him a long look, which said a great deal.

When he stood up, he must have felt weak, because his body seemed to sway a little. But he was still quite calm. His features were expressionless once more. He began by asking a question. The magistrate looked at Maigret as if waiting for him to answer.

"He asks if he may keep this letter?"

"I would rather it were photographed first. It won't take more than a few minutes. We can send it up to the Criminal Records Office . . ."

Translation. Clark appeared to understand, nodded his head, and handed the letter to the clerk, who bore it off. Then he went on talking. It was maddening not to be able to understand. The shortest speech seemed to go on for ever and the superintendent kept wanting to interrupt to ask what he was saying.

"First of all, he wants to consult his solicitor, because what he has just learnt was totally unexpected and it changes everything . . ."

Why did Maigret feel moved at these words? At this great healthy man who three days before had been riding on roundabouts with Ellen, and only a few hours before had been dancing the tango in a haze of blue light . . . and who had now received a much more shattering blow than the one he had dealt the superintendent . . . And, like Maigret, he had barely flinched . . . He had sworn briefly . . . Banged his fist on the table . . . Remained silent for a while . . .

"Well . . . Well! . . ."

It was a pity they couldn't understand each other. Maigret would have liked to have been able to talk to him.

"What's he saying now?"

"That he now wants to offer a reward of a thousand dollars to the police officer who discovers the murderer . . ."

While this was translated, Clark looked at Maigret as if to say: "You see what a good sport I am . . ."

"Tell him, that if we win them, the thousand dollars will go to the police orphanage . . ."

It was odd. It was as though they were now competing to see who could be most polite. Clark listened to the interpreter, and nodded.

"Well . . ."

Then he began speaking again, this time in the tone of a businessman conducting his affairs.

"He supposes—but he doesn't want to do anything before having seen his solicitor—that an interview between him and this man—Prosper Donge—will be necessary . . . He asks if he might be permitted to do this and if . . ."

It was the magistrate's turn to nod gravely. And in another minute they would all have been exchanging compliments.

"After you . . ."

"Please . . ."

"No, really . . ."

Clark then asked some more questions, turning frequently to Maigret.

"He wants to know, sir, what will happen about the punch-up, and if there will be any repercussions. He doesn't know what consequences such an act might have in France . . . In his country . . ."

"Well, tell him I have no recollection of the event he mentions . . ."

The magistrate looked anxiously towards the door. It was too good to be true! He was afraid some new incident would come to disturb this marvellous harmony. If only they would hurry up and bring back the letter which . . .

They waited. In silence. They had nothing more to say to each other. Clark lit another cigarette, after having signed to Maigret to lend him his matches.

At last the clerk came back with the dreaded piece of blue paper.

"It's been copied, sir . . . May I?"

"Yes, give the letter to Monsieur Clark . . ."

Clark slipped it carefully into his wallet, put the wallet in his breast pocket, and forgetting he had come without his hat, looked round for it on the chairs. Then he remembered, smiled stiffly and said goodnight to them all.

When the interpreter had also gone, and the door was shut, Monsieur Bonneau coughed two or three times, walked round his desk, and picked up some papers which he then didn't know what to do with.

"Hum! . . . Was that what you wanted to happen, superintendent?"

"What do you think, sir?"

"I believe it is I who am asking the questions."

"I'm so sorry . . . Of course! You see, I have the feeling

that it won't be long before Monsieur Clark remarries . . .
And the child is definitely Donge's son . . ."

"The son of a man who is in prison and who is ac-
cused of . . ."

". . . various crimes, yes," Maigret sighed. "But the boy
is nevertheless his son. What can I do under the circumstances . . ."

He, too, looked for his hat, which he had left at the
Majestic. He felt very odd leaving the Palais de Justice
without it, so he took a taxi back to the Boulevard
Richard-Lenoir.

The bruise on his chin had had time to turn black.
Madame Maigret spotted it at once.

"You've been fighting again!" she said, laying the table.
"And, of course, you're minus a hat! . . . What was it this
time? . . ."

He felt satisfied, and smiled broadly as he took his
table-napkin out of its silver ring.

8

MAIGRET DOZING

And it wasn't at all bad either to be sitting comfortably at his desk, with the stove purring away at his back, and the window on the left curtained with lace-like morning mist, while in front of him was the black marble Louis-Philippe mantelpiece, the hands of the clock permanently stuck at noon for the last twenty years; on the wall a photograph in a black and gilt frame of a group of gentlemen in frock-coats and top hats, with improbable moustaches and pointed beards: the association of secretaries of the Central Police Station, when Maigret was twenty-four!

Four pipes arranged in order of size on his desk.

A RICH AMERICAN WOMAN STRANGLED IN
THE BASEMENT OF THE MAJESTIC.

The headline ran across the front page of an evening paper of the day before. To journalists, of course, all American women are always rich. But Maigret's smile broadened on seeing a photograph of himself, in his overcoat and bowler hat, and with his pipe in his mouth, looking down at something which wasn't shown in the picture.

SUPERINTENDENT MAIGRET
EXAMINES THE CORPSE.

But it was a photograph which had been taken a year before, in the Bois de Boulogne, when he had in fact been looking at the body of a Russian who had been shot with a revolver.

Some more important documents, in manila folders.

Report from Inspector Torrence as to inquiry regarding Monsieur Edgar Fagonet, alias Eusebio Fualdès, alias Zebio, aged twenty-four, born in Lille.

"Son of Fagonet, Albert Jean-Marie, foreman at the Lecoeur Works, deceased three years ago;

". . . and Jeanne Albertine Octavie Hautbois, wife of the above, aged 54, housewife.

"The following information was given to us, either by the concierge at no. 57 Rue Caulaincourt, where Edgar Fagonet lives with his mother and sister, or by neighbours and shopkeepers in the area, or on the telephone by the Police Station in the Gasworks district of Lille.

"We have also been in touch by telephone with the 'Chevalet Sanatorium' in Megève, and have personally seen the manager of the Imperia cinema, in the Boulevard des Capucines.

"Although opinion must be reserved until further verification has been carried out, the information below appears to be correct.

"The Fagonet family, of Lille, led a decent life, and occupied a bungalow in the modern part of the Gasworks district. It appears that the parents' ambition was to give Edgar Fagonet a good education, and in fact the latter went to the Lycée at the age of eleven.

"Shortly afterwards he had to leave it for a year to go to a sanatorium on the island of Oléron. His health then apparently restored, he continued his studies, but they were constantly interrupted from that time on owing to his weak constitution.

"When he was seventeen, it was found necessary to send him to a high altitude, and he spent four years at the Chevalet Sanatorium, near Megève.

"Doctor Chevalet remembers Fagonet well; he was a very good-looking boy and had a lot of success with certain of the female patients. He had several affairs while he was there. It was also there that he became an accomplished dancer, because the rules at the establishment were very informal, and it appears that in general the patients were intent upon pleasure.

"Turned down permanently by the recruiting board.

"At twenty-one, Fagonet returned to Lille, just in time to close his father's eyes. The father left a few small savings, but not enough to feed his family.

"Fagonet's sister, Émilie, aged nineteen, has a bone disorder which renders her virtually disabled. Additionally, she is of below average intelligence, and needs constant care.

"It appears that at this time Edgar Fagonet made serious attempts to find regular employment, first in Lille and then in Roubaix. Unfortunately his interrupted education was a handicap. On the other hand, although cured, his constitution prevented him from doing manual labour.

"It was then that he came to Paris, where he could be found a few weeks later in a sky-blue uniform, working at the Imperia cinema, which was the first to employ young men instead of usherettes, and which also took on a number of poor students.

"It is difficult to get precise information on this point because those involved have proved discreet, but it appears certain that many of these young men, shown to advantage in their uniforms, made FRUITFUL conquests at the Imperia!"

Maigret grinned because Torrence had found it necessary to underline the word "fruitful" in red ink.

"At any rate one of Fagonet's first acts—his friends were now beginning to call him Zebio, because of his Latin-American appearance—was to bring his mother and sister to Paris and install them in a three-room flat, in the Rue Caulaincourt.

"He is considered by the concierge and by neighbours to be a particularly dutiful son, and it is often he who goes out to do the shopping in the mornings.

"It was through colleagues at the Imperia that he learnt, about a year ago, that the Majestic was looking for a professional dancing-partner for its tea-room. He applied, and was taken on after a few days' trial. He then adopted the name Eusebio Fualdès, and the hotel management have no complaints to make on his account.

"According to the staff, he is a rather timid, sentimental and shy boy. Some of them call him 'a proper girl.'

"He doesn't talk much, and conserves his strength, because he's apt to have relapses and has several times had to go and lie down on a bed in the basement, especially when he has had to stay late because of gala evenings.

"Although he gets on well with everyone, he doesn't seem to have any friends and is not much inclined towards gossip.

"It is thought that his monthly earnings, including tips, must be in the region of two thousand to two thousand five hundred francs.

"That just about sums up life in the household in the Rue Caulaincourt.

"Edgar Fagonet doesn't drink, doesn't smoke, and doesn't take any drugs. His poor health prevents him doing so.

"His mother is a woman from the North of France— stocky and energetic. She has often spoken—to the concierge for one—about getting a job herself, but the fact that she has to look after her daughter has always prevented this.

"We have tried to find out if Fagonet has ever been to the Côte d'Azur. We can't get any precise information on this point. Some say he stayed there for a few days, about three or four years ago, while he was still at the Imperia, with a middle-aged woman. But the information is too vague to be admitted as evidence."

———

Maigret slowly filled pipe no. 3, filled the stove, and went to have a look at the Seine, which was tinged with gold by a pale winter sun. Then he sighed comfortably and sat down again.

Report by Inspector Lucas concerning Ramuel, Jean Oscar Adelbert, aged forty-eight, living in a furnished flat at no. 14 Rue Delambre (XIVe).

"Ramuel was born in Nice, of a French father, now deceased, and an Italian mother, whom we cannot trace and who seems to have gone back to her own country some time ago. His father was a market-gardener.

"At eighteen, Jean Ramuel was bookkeeper to a wholesaler in Les Halles in Paris, but we have been unable to get precise information about this, because the merchant died ten years ago.

"Enlisted voluntarily at nineteen. Left the army with the rank of quartermaster-sergeant at twenty-four and entered the service of a broker whom he left almost immediately to work as junior accounts clerk in a sugar refinery in Egypt.

"He stayed there three years, came back to France, took various jobs in the city sector of Paris and tried his luck on the Stock Exchange.

"At thirty-two, he embarked for Guayaquil, in Ecuador, to work for a Franco-English mining company. He was commissioned to go and sort out the accounts, which seemed to be in a mess.

"He was away for six years. It was there that he met Marie Deligeard, on whom we have little information and who was most probably engaged in a somewhat disreputable profession in Central America.

"He returned with her. The company headquarters having been transferred to London, we have little information about this period.

"The couple then lived for some time fairly comfortably in Toulon, Cassis and Marseilles. Ramuel tried his hand at some property and land deals, but didn't have much success.

"Marie Deligeard, whom he introduces as Madame Ramuel, although they aren't married, is a loud-mouthed, vulgar woman who is quite prepared to make scenes in public and who takes a malicious pleasure in making a spectacle of herself.

"They have frequent rows. Sometimes Ramuel leaves his companion for several days, but it's always she who has the last word.

"Ramuel and Marie Deligeard then came to Paris, and took quite a comfortable furnished flat in the Rue Delambre: bedroom, kitchen, bathroom and hall, at a rent of eight hundred francs a month.

"Ramuel took a job as an accountant in the Atoum Bank, in the Rue Caumartin. (The bank has now crashed, but Atoum has started a carpet business in the Rue des Saints-Pères, in the name of one of his employees.)

"Ramuel left the bank before the crash, and almost immediately saw an advertisement and applied for the post of bookkeeper at the Majestic.

"He has been there three years. The management are quite satisfied with him. The staff don't like him, because he's excessively strict.

"On several occasions, when he's had a tiff with his companion, he has stayed for days at the hotel without going home, sleeping on a makeshift bed. He has nearly always had telephone calls on these occasions, or else the woman has come to fetch him from the basement herself.

"The staff can't believe their eyes, because she seems to inspire absolute terror in him.

"Note that Jean Ramuel returned to the communal life in the flat in the Rue Delambre yesterday."

A quarter of an hour later, the old usher knocked softly on Maigret's door. Receiving no answer, he pushed the door quietly open and crept in on tiptoe.

The superintendent seemed to be asleep. He was sprawled in his chair, with his waistcoat unbuttoned and a burnt-out pipe in his mouth.

The usher was about to cough to let him know he was there when Maigret mumbled, without opening his eyes:

"What is it?"

"A gentleman to see you . . . Here's his card."

Maigret still seemed reluctant to shake off his drowsiness and he stretched out his hand without opening his eyes. Then he sighed and, putting the visiting card down on his desk, picked up the telephone.

"Shall I bring him in?"

"In a minute . . ."

He had barely glanced at the card: ÉTIENNE JOLIVET, ASSISTANT MANAGER OF CRÉDIT LYONNAIS, O BRANCH.

"Hello! . . . Would you ask Monsieur Bonneau, the examining magistrate, to be good enough to give me the name and address of Monsieur Clark's solicitor . . . Solicitor . . . yes . . . that's right . . . Then get him for me on the telephone . . . It's urgent . . ."

For more than quarter of an hour, the dapper Monsieur Jolivet, in striped trousers, black jacket and hat as rigid as reinforced concrete, remained sitting very upright on the edge of his chair, in the gloomy waiting-room at Police Headquarters. His companions were an evil-looking youth and a streetwalker who was recounting her adventures in a raucous voice.

". . . For a start, how could I have taken his wallet, without him noticing? . . . These provincials are all the same . . . They daren't tell their wives what they've spent in Paris and so they pretend they've been robbed . . . It's lucky the vice squad superintendent knows me . . . That's proof that . . ."

"Hello! . . . Monsieur Herbert Davidson? . . . How do you do, Monsieur Herbert Davidson. Superintendent Maigret here . . . Yes . . . I had the pleasure of meeting your client Monsieur Clark yesterday . . . He was most kind . . . What's that? . . . No . . . not at all! . . . I've forgotten all about it . . . I'm telephoning because I got the impression that he was prepared to help us in so far as he was able . . . You say he's with you at the moment? . . .

"Could you ask him . . . Hello! . . . I know that in the circles he moves in, particularly in the United States, the partners in a marriage lead fairly separate lives . . . Nevertheless he may have noticed . . . No, just a minute . . . Wait, Monsieur Davidson, you can translate for him afterwards . . . We know that Mrs. Clark received at least three letters from Paris during the last few years . . . I want to know if Monsieur Clark saw them . . . And I also particularly want to know if by any chance she received any more letters of the same kind . . . Yes . . . I'll hang on . . . thank you . . ."

And he heard a murmur of voices at the other end of the line.

"Hello! . . . Yes? . . . He didn't open them? . . . He didn't ask his wife what they were? . . . Naturally! How very strange . . ."

He would like to see Madame Maigret getting letters without showing them to him!

"About one every three months? . . . Always in the same handwriting? . . . Yes . . . A Paris postmark? . . . Just a minute, Monsieur Davidson . . ."

He went and opened the door of the inspectors' room, because they were making a terrible noise.

"Shut up, you lot!"

Then he came back.

"Hello! . . . Fairly substantial sums? . . . Would you be good enough, Monsieur Davidson, to make a written note of these details and send it to the examining magistrate? . . . No! Nothing else . . . I apologize . . . I don't know how the papers got hold of it, but I can assure you I had nothing to do with it . . . Only this morning I sent away four journalists and two photographers who had been lying in wait for me in the corridor at Police Headquarters. Please give my regards to Monsieur Clark . . ."

He frowned. When he had opened the door of the inspectors' room just now, he had thought he recognized? . . . He looked in again, and there, sitting on the table, were a reporter and his photographer colleague.

"Listen, my young friend . . . I think I was shouting loud enough for you to hear just now . . . If a single word of what I said appears in your rag, you'll never get another scrap of information out of me . . . Understand?"

But he was half smiling as he went back to his room and rang for the usher.

"Bring in Monsieur . . . Monsieur Jolivet . . ."

"Good morning, superintendent . . . Forgive me for bothering you . . . I thought I ought . . . When I read the paper yesterday evening . . ."

"Please sit down . . ."

"I should add that I didn't come here on my own initiative, but after consultation with our head manager, who I telephoned first thing this morning . . . The name Prosper Donge struck me, because I happened to have seen the name somewhere recently . . . I should explain that it's my job at the O Branch to pass the cheques . . . They go through automatically, of course, because the customer's account has been checked previously . . . I just glance at them . . . Attach my stamp . . . However, as a large sum of money was involved . . ."

"Just a minute . . . Do you mean Prosper Donge was a customer of yours?"

"He had been for five years, superintendent. And before that, even, because his account was transferred to us at the beginning of that period by our Cannes branch . . ."

"Can I ask you a few questions . . . It will make it easier for me to get my ideas in order . . . Prosper Donge was a customer at your Cannes branch . . . Can you tell me the size of his account at that date?"

"A very modest account, like that of most of the hotel employees who are customers of ours . . . However, one must remember that as they get their board and lodging free, if they are careful, they can put aside the greater part of their earnings . . . It was so in Donge's case and he paid about a thousand to fifteen hundred francs into his account each month . . .

"In addition to that, he had just got twenty thousand francs from a bond he had asked us to buy for him . . . So in fact he had about fifty-five thousand francs on arrival in Paris . . ."

"And he went on paying in small amounts?"

"Well—I've brought a list of his transactions with me. There's something very worrying about it, as you will see . . . The first year, Donge, who was living in a flat in the Rue Bray, near the Étoile, paid in about another twelve thousand francs . . .

"The second year, he made withdrawals and didn't pay in. He changed his address. He went to live in Saint-Cloud, where I gathered from the cheques he wrote, he was having a house built . . . Cheques to the estate agent, to the carpenter, to the decorators, to the builders . . .

"So by the end of that year, as you can see from this statement, he only had eight hundred and thirty-three francs and a few centimes left in his account . . .

"Then, three years ago, that is a few months later . . ."

"Excuse me— You said *three years ago* . . . ?"

"That's right . . . I'll give you the exact dates in a minute . . . Three years ago, he sent a letter notifying us that he had moved and asking us to note his new address: 117b Rue Réaumur . . ."

"Just a minute . . . Have you ever seen Donge in person?"

"I may have seen him, but I don't remember . . . I'm not at the counter. I have a private office where I only see the public through a sort of spy-hole . . ."

"Have your employees seen him?"

"I asked several of the staff that this morning . . . One of the clerks remembers him, because he was also having a house built in the suburbs . . . He told me he remembered remarking that Donge had left his house almost before it had been built . . ."

"Could you telephone this man?"

He did so. Maigret took the opportunity of stretching, like someone who is still half asleep, but his eyes were alert.

"You were saying . . . Let me see . . . Donge changed his address and went to live at 117b Rue Réaumur . . . Will you excuse me a moment?"

He disappeared in the direction of the inspectors' office.

"Lucas . . . Jump in a taxi . . . 117b Rue Réaumur . . . Find out all you can about Monsieur Prosper Donge . . . I'll explain later . . ."

He came back to the assistant branch manager.

"What transactions did Donge make after that?"

"It's that that I wanted to see you about. I was horrified, this morning, when I looked at his account, and even more horrified when I saw the last entry . . . The first American cheque . . ."

"Excuse me—the what?"

"Oh—there were several! The first American cheque, drawn on a bank in Detroit and made out to Prosper Donge, was dated March, three years ago, and was for five hundred dollars . . . I can tell you what that was worth, exactly, at the time . . ."

"It doesn't matter!"

"The cheque was paid into his account. Six months later another cheque for the same amount was sent to us by Donge, asking us to pay it in and credit it to his account . . ."

The assistant manager suddenly became worried by the superintendent's complacent expression, and the fact that he no longer appeared to be listening to him. And Maigret's thoughts were far away. It had suddenly occurred to him that if he hadn't telephoned the solicitor before seeing his visitor, if he hadn't asked certain questions when he was speaking to him, it would all have looked as though it was sheer chance . . .

"I'm listening, Monsieur—Monsieur Jolivet isn't it?"

He had to look at the visiting card each time he said it.

"Or rather, I already know what you are going to tell me. Donge continued to receive cheques from Detroit, at the rate of about one every three months . . ."

"That is correct . . . But . . ."

"The cheques amounted to how much altogether?"

"Three hundred thousand francs . . ."

"Which remained in the bank without Donge ever drawing any money out?"

"Yes . . . But for the last eight months, there has been no cheque . . ."

Ah! Hadn't Mrs. Clark been on a cruise in the Pacific, with her son, before coming to France?

"During this time, did Donge continue to pay small amounts into his account?"

"I can't find any trace of any . . . Of course any such payments would have been derisory compared with the cheques from America . . . But I'm just coming to the worrying part . . . The letter the day before yesterday . . . It wasn't me who dealt with it . . . It was the head of the foreign currency department—you'll see why in a minute . . . Well, we got this letter from Donge the day before yesterday . . . Instead of containing a cheque as usual, it asked us to make one out for him, payable to the bearer, at a bank in Brussels . . . It's a common procedure . . . People going abroad often ask us to give them a cheque payable at another bank, which avoids complications with letters of credit and also avoids the necessity of carrying large sums in cash . . ."

"How much was the cheque for?"

"Two hundred and eighty thousand French francs . . . Nearly all the money in his account . . . In fact there is now only a little under twenty thousand francs in Donge's account . . ."

"You made out the cheque?"

"We sent it to the address he gave, as requested . . ."

"Which was?"

"Monsieur Prosper Donge, 117b Rue Réaumur, as usual . . ."

"So the letter would have been delivered yesterday morning?"

"Probably . . . But in that case, Donge can't be in possession of it . . ."

And the assistant manager brandished the newspaper.

"He can't have got it, because, the day before yesterday, at just about the time when we were making out the cheque, Prosper Donge was arrested!"

Maigret leafed rapidly through the telephone directory and discovered that 117b Rue Réaumur, where there were several numbers, also had a telephone in the concierge's lodge. He dialled the number. Lucas had arrived there a few minutes earlier.

He gave him brief instructions.

"A letter, yes, addressed to Donge . . . The envelope is stamped with the address of the O Branch of the Crédit Lyonnais . . . Hurry, old chap . . . Call me back . . ."

"I think, superintendent," said the assistant branch manager solemnly, "I did right to . . ."

"Yes! Yes!"

But he no longer saw the poor fellow, and paid not the slightest attention to him. He was miles away, as if in a dream, and had to keep moving objects about, stirring up the stove, walking to and fro.

"An employee from the Crédit Lyonnais, sir . . ."

"Tell him to come in . . ."

As he spoke, the telephone rang. The bank clerk remained standing nervously in the doorway, staring at his assistant manager in horror, wondering what he could possibly have done to be summoned to the Quai des Orfèvres.

"Lucas?"

"Well, chief, the building isn't a residential block. It's only offices, most of them with only one room. Some of them are rented by provincial businessmen who find it useful to have a Paris address. Some of them practically never set foot in the place and their mail is forwarded on to them. Others have a typist to answer the telephone . . . Hello! . . ."

"Go on."

"Three years ago, Donge had an office here for two months, at a rent of six hundred francs a month . . . He only came here two or three times . . . Since then he has sent a hundred francs to the concierge each month to forward his mail . . ."

"Where is it forwarded to? . . ."

"Poste Restante to the Jem bureau, 42 Boulevard Haussmann . . ."

"To what name?"

"The envelopes are ready typed and Donge sends them in advance . . . Wait—it's a bit dark in the lodge . . . Yes, put the light on, mate . . . Here we are . . . J. M. D. Poste Restante, Jem, 42 Boulevard Haussmann . . . That's all . . .

Private bureaux are allowed to accept letters addressed with initials only . . ."

"Did you keep your taxi? . . . No? . . . Idiot! Jump in a cab . . . What time is it? . . . Eleven . . . Get over to the Boulevard Haussmann . . . Did the concierge send on a letter yesterday morning? . . . He did? . . . Hurry, then . . ."

He had forgotten the two men, who didn't know what to do and were listening in bewilderment. His thoughts had raced ahead so fast that he almost found himself asking: "What are you two still doing here?"

Then he suddenly calmed down.

"What do you do at the bank?" he asked the clerk, who started in surprise.

"I'm on current accounts."

"Do you know Prosper Donge?"

"Yes, I know him . . . That is, I've seen him several times . . . You see he was having a house built in the suburbs at one time, and so was I . . . Only I chose a plot of land at . . ."

"Yes—I know . . . Go on . . ."

"He used to come in from time to time to draw out small amounts for the workmen who didn't have bank accounts and wouldn't accept cheques . . . He found it very tiresome . . . I remember we discussed it . . . We said everyone should have a bank account as they do in America . . . It was difficult for him to get there, because he had to be at the Majestic from six in the morning until six at night, and the bank was shut by then . . . I told him . . . the assistant manager won't mind, because we do it for some of our

customers . . . that he could just telephone me and that I
would send him the money to be signed for on receipt . . . I
sent him money like that to the Majestic two or three
times . . ."

"Have you seen him since?"

"I don't think so . . . But I had to go to Étretat for two
summers running, to run the branch there . . . He could
have come in then . . ."

Maigret pulled open a drawer of his desk, took out a
photograph of Donge and laid it on the desk without
saying a word.

"That's him!" said the bank clerk. "You couldn't miss
his face. It appears—so he told me—that he had smallpox
as a child and the farm people he was living with didn't
even call in a doctor . . ."

"Are you sure that's him?"

"As sure as I am of anything!"

"And you'd recognize his writing?"

"I would certainly recognize it," the assistant manager
put in, annoyed at being relegated to second place.

Maigret handed them various bits of paper, with
writing by different people on them.

"No! . . . No! . . . That's not his writing . . . Ah! . . . Wait
a minute . . . There's one of his 7s . . . He had a very char-
acteristic way of writing his 7s . . . And his Fs too . . .
That's one of his Fs . . ."

The writing they were pointing at was indeed Donge's;
it was one of the slips he scrawled when people ordered so
many coffees, coffee with croissants, tea, portions of toast
or cups of chocolate.

The telephone remained silent. It was just midday.

"Well, thank you very much, gentlemen!"

What on earth was Lucas doing at the Jem bureau? He was quite capable of having taken a bus, to save the taxi fare!

9

MONSIEUR CHARLES'S NEWSPAPER

Apart, they might still have passed. But standing together by the entrance to Police Headquarters, they looked as if they were waiting at a factory gate, and made a pathetic, grotesque pair. Gigi perched on her thin legs, in her worn rabbit-skin coat, her eyes wary, defying the policeman on duty at the entrance and peering to see who it was whenever she heard anyone coming; and poor Charlotte, who hadn't had the heart to do her hair or put on make-up, with her large moon-like face blotched and red because she'd been crying and was still sniffling. Her nose was bright red, and looked like a small red ball in the middle of her face.

She was wearing a decent black cloth coat, with an astrakhan collar and band of astrakhan round the hem. She held limply on to a large glacé kid bag. Without the ghoulish presence of Gigi, and the red gleaming in the middle of her face, she might have looked fairly presentable.

"There he is!"

Charlotte hadn't budged, but Gigi had been walking frenziedly to and fro. And now she had seen Maigret arriving, with a colleague. Too late, he saw the two women.

It was sunny out on the quay, with a touch of spring in the air.

"Excuse me, superintendent . . ."

He shook hands with his colleague . . .

"Have a good lunch, old chap . . ."

"Can we talk to you for a minute, superintendent?"

And Charlotte burst into tears, stuffing her handkerchief which was rolled in a ball into her mouth. People in the street turned round. Maigret waited patiently. Gigi said, as if to excuse her friend: "The magistrate sent for her and she's just been seeing him . . ."

Oh dear—Monsieur Bonneau. He had a right to do so, of course. But all the same . . .

"Is it true, sir, that Prosper has . . . has admitted everything?"

This time Maigret smiled openly. Was that all the magistrate had been able to think up? That corny trick used by junior policemen? And that great goose Charlotte had believed him!

"It's not true, is it? I knew it wasn't! If you knew what he said to me! . . . To listen to him you'd think I was the lowest of the low . . ."

The policeman on duty at the entrance was looking at them with amusement. It was a curious sight—Maigret besieged by the two women, one of them crying and the other peering at him with no attempt to hide her antagonism.

"As if I'd write an anonymous letter accusing Prosper, when I'm sure he didn't kill her! . . . If it had been a revolver, now, I might just have believed it . . . But not strangling someone . . . And particularly not doing it again the next day to some poor man who hadn't done anything . . . Have you discovered anything else, then, superintendent? Do you think they'll keep him in prison?"

Maigret signed to a taxi which was passing.

"Get in!" he told the two women. "I was going on an errand—you can come with me . . ."

It was quite true. He had at last had a telephone call from Lucas, who had drawn a blank at the Jem bureau. He had asked him to meet him in the Boulevard Haussmann. And he had just had the idea that he might . . .

Both the women tried to sit on the flap seats, but he made them sit on the back seat and he himself sat with his back to the driver. It was one of the first fine days of the year. The streets of Paris lay gleaming in the sun, and everyone looked more cheerful.

"Tell me, Charlotte, is Donge still paying his savings into the bank?"

He felt irritated with Gigi, who frowned each time he opened his mouth, as if suspecting a trap. She was clearly longing to say to her friend: "Look out! . . . Think before you answer . . ."

But Charlotte exclaimed: "Savings! Poor love! . . . We haven't saved anything for a long time now! . . . Since we've had this house weighing us down, and that's a fact! . . . It was supposed to cost forty thousand francs at the most, according to the estimates . . . First the foundations cost three times as much as they expected, because they found a subterranean stream . . . Then, when the

walls were being built, there was a building strike which
brought everything to a stop just as winter began . . . Five
thousand francs here . . . Three thousand francs there . . .
They fleeced us on all sides! If I told you how much the
house had cost us to date you wouldn't believe it! I don't
know the exact figure, but it must be more than eighty
thousand, and there are still some things which haven't
been paid for . . ."

"So Donge hasn't any money in the bank?"

"He hasn't even got an account . . . He hasn't had one
for . . . wait a minute . . . for about three years now . . . I
remember because one day the postman brought a money
order for about eight hundred francs . . . I didn't know
what it was . . . When Donge got back he told me he had
written to the bank to close his account . . ."

"You can't remember the date?"

"What's that got to do with you?" asked Gigi, who
couldn't refrain from adding her sour note.

"I know it was in the winter, because I was busy breaking the ice round the pump when the postman came . . .
Wait . . . I went to the market in Saint-Cloud that day . . . I
bought a goose . . . So it must have been a few days before
Christmas . . ."

"Where are we going?" grumbled Gigi, looking out of
the window.

Just at that moment, the taxi stopped in the Boulevard
Haussmann, just before the Faubourg Saint-Honoré. Lucas
was standing on the pavement and goggled as he saw
Maigret follow the two women out of the cab.

"Wait a second . . ." the superintendent told them.

He drew Lucas aside.

"Well?"

"Look . . . You see that sort of narrow shop, between the suitcase shop and the ladies' hairdresser? That's the Jem bureau . . . It's run by a revolting old man whom I couldn't get any information from . . . He wanted to shut the bureau and go off to lunch, pretending it was his lunch hour . . . I forced him to stay . . . He's furious . . . He insists that I've no right without a warrant . . ."

Maigret went into the shop, which was so poorly lit it was almost dark, and cut in two by a dirty wooden counter. Small wooden pigeon-holes, also filthy, lined the walls and these were full of letters.

"I'd like to know . . ." the old man began.

"I'll ask the questions, if you don't mind," Maigret growled. "You get letters addressed by initials, I believe, which is not allowed by the official poste restante, so your clientele must be a pretty bunch . . ."

"I pay my licence," the old man promptly objected.

He wore glasses with heavy lenses, behind which darted rheumy eyes. His jacket was dirty and the collar of his shirt frayed and greasy. A rancid smell emanated from his body and filled the whole shop.

"I want to know if you have a register where you note the real name of your clients against the initials . . ."

The man snickered.

"D'you think they'd come here if they had to give their names? . . . Why not ask them for identity papers?"

It was somewhat unpleasant to think of pretty women coming furtively into the shop, which had served as a go-between for so many adulterous couples, and many other shady transactions.

"You got a letter yesterday morning addressed with the initials J. M. D. . . ."

"It's possible. I've already said so to your colleague. He even insisted on checking that the letter was no longer here . . ."

"So, someone came to collect it. Can you tell me when?"

"I've no idea, and even if I had, I doubt if I'd tell you . . ."

"You realize I may come and close down your shop one of these days?"

"Other people have said the same to me, and my shop, as you call it, has been here for the last forty-two years . . . If I counted up all the husbands who've come to shout at me, and who've even threatened me with their sticks . . ."

Lucas had been quite right in saying he was revolting.

"If it's all the same to you, I'll put up the shutters and go and have my lunch . . ."

Where could the old brute possibly have lunch? Surely he hadn't got a family—wife and children? It seemed far more likely that he was a bachelor, with his special place at some dingy restaurant in the neighbourhood, with his napkin in a ring.

"Have you ever seen this man?"

Maigret refusing to be hustled, produced Donge's photograph again, and curiosity gained the upper hand over the man's ill humour. He bent to peer at it and had to hold it within a few centimetres of his face. His expression didn't change. He shrugged.

"I don't remember seeing him . . ." he mumbled, as if disappointed.

The two women were waiting outside, in front of the narrow shop window. Maigret called Charlotte in.

"And do you recognize her?"

If Charlotte was acting, she was doing it remarkably well; she was looking round as if shocked and embarrassed, which was hardly surprising in such surroundings.

"What is . . . ?" she began.

She was terrified. Why had she been brought here? She looked round instinctively for Gigi, who came in of her own accord.

"How many people are you going to bring in here then?"

"You don't recognize either of them? You can't tell me whether it was a man or a woman who came to collect the letter addressed to J. M. D., or when the letter was collected?"

Without replying, the man seized a wooden shutter and started to hang it in front of the door. There was no option but to beat a hasty retreat. Maigret, Lucas and the two women found themselves outside on the pavement, under the chestnut trees with their new spring buds.

"You two can go now! . . ."

He watched them go off. Gigi had barely gone ten metres before she started violently haranguing her companion whom she was dragging along at a pace little suited to Charlotte's dumpy figure.

"Any news, chief?"

What could Maigret say? He was brooding, anxious. The spring weather seemed to make him irritable rather than relaxed.

"I don't know . . . Look . . . Go and have some lunch . . . Stay in the office this afternoon . . . Tell the banks—in France and Brussels—that if a cheque for two hundred and eighty thousand francs has been presented . . ."

He was only a few metres from the Majestic. He went down the Rue de Ponthieu, and into the bar near the staff door of the hotel. They served snacks there and he ordered some tinned cassoulet, which he ate morosely, alone at a little table at the back, near two men who were hurriedly downing a snack before going to the races and who were talking about horses.

Anyone who followed him that afternoon, would have been hard put to it to decide what exactly he was doing. Having finished his meal, he had some coffee, bought some tobacco and filled his pouch. Then he went out of the bar and stood on the pavement for a while, looking around.

He probably hadn't formulated any precise plan of action. He ambled slowly into the Majestic and along the back corridor, and stood by the clocking-on machine, rather like a traveller with hours to wait at a station, putting coins into the chocolate machines.

People brushed past him, mostly cooks, with cloths round their necks, nipping out to have a quick drink at the bar next door.

As he went farther along the corridor, the heat grew more intense, and there was a strong smell of cooking.

The cloakroom was empty. He washed his hands at a basin, for no reason, to pass the time, and spent a good ten minutes cleaning his nails. Then, as he was too hot, he took off his overcoat and hung it in locker 89.

Jean Ramuel was sitting in state in his glass cage. In the still-room opposite, the three women were working at an accelerated pace, with a new cook in a white jacket who had replaced Prosper.

"Who's that?" Maigret asked Ramuel.

"A temp, whom they've engaged until they find some-one . . . He's called Monsieur Charles . . . So you've come to take a little stroll round, superintendent? . . . Excuse me a minute . . ."

It was hectic. The luxury clientele ate late, and the chits were piling up in front of Ramuel, waiters were dash-ing past, all the telephones were ringing at once and the service-lifts were shooting up and down non-stop.

Maigret, still wearing his bowler, wandered about with his hands in his pockets, stopping by a cook who was thickening a sauce as if it fascinated him, watching the women wash up, or peering through the glass partitions into the guests' servants' hall.

He went up the back stairs, as he had done on his first visit, but stopped on all the floors this time, without hurrying, and still looking rather disgruntled. As he went down again, he was joined by the manager, who was out of breath.

"They've just told me you were here, superintendent . . . I don't suppose you've had lunch? . . . May I offer . . ."

"I've eaten, thank you . . ."

"May I inquire if you've any news? . . . I was so taken aback when they arrested that Prosper Donge . . . But are you sure you won't have anything? . . . A brandy, perhaps? . . ."

The manager was growing more and more embarrassed, finding himself on the narrow staircase with Maigret, who obstinately refused to show any reaction. At times the superintendent seemed as slumberous and thick-skinned as a pachyderm.

"I had hoped the press wouldn't get on to the affair . . . You know, for a hotel, what . . . As for Donge . . ."

It was hopeless. Maigret offered him no help as he stumbled on. He had started going downstairs again, and they had now reached the basement.

"A man I would have cited as of exemplary character, only a few days ago . . . Because as you can imagine, we get all sorts in a hotel like this . . ."

Maigret was glancing from one glass partition to another, or as he would say, from one aquarium to another. They finally ended up in the cloakroom, by the famous locker 89, where two human lives had come definitely to an end.

"As for that poor Colleboeuf . . . Forgive me if I'm boring you . . . I've just thought of something . . . Don't you think it would need unusual strength to strangle a man in broad daylight, only a few metres from numerous people—I mean so that the victim had no chance to cry out or struggle? . . . It would be possible now, because every-one's rushing about making a din . . . But at half past four or five in the afternoon . . ."

"You were in the middle of lunch, I imagine?" Maigret murmured.

"It doesn't matter . . . We're used to eating when we can . . ."

"Do please go and finish your meal . . . I'm just go-ing . . . I'll just see . . . If you'll excuse me . . ."

And he ambled off down the passage again, opening and shutting doors, and lighting his pipe, which he then allowed to go out.

His steps kept bringing him back to the still-room, and he began to know the occupants' every movement, and muttered between his teeth: "So . . . Donge is there . . . He's there from six o'clock onwards every day . . . Good . . . He had a cup of coffee at home, which Charlotte prepared when she got in . . . OK then . . . When he gets here, I imagine he pours himself a cup as soon as the first percolator's hot . . . Yes . . ."

Did it make any sense?

"He usually takes a cup of coffee up to the night porter . . . Yes . . . In fact, that day, it was probably because it was already after ten past six and Donge still hadn't come up that Justin Colleboeuf came down . . . So . . . Well . . . for that or some other reason . . . Hmm!"

In fact they weren't filling the silver coffee-pots that had been used at breakfast, but little brown glazed pots, each with a tiny filter on top.

". . . Breakfasts go up all morning, more and more of them . . . OK . . . Then Donge has a bit to eat himself . . . They bring him something on a tray . . ."

"Would you mind moving a little to the right or left, superintendent? . . . You're blocking my view of the trays . . ."

It was Ramuel, who had to oversee everything from his glass cage. He even had to count all the cups leaving the still-room as well, then?

"I'm so sorry to have to ask you . . ."

"Not a bit! Not a bit!"

Three o'clock. The pace slackened a bit. One of the cooks had just fetched his coat to go out.

"If anyone wants me, Ramuel, I'll be back at five . . . I've got to go to the tax office . . ."

Nearly all the little brown coffee-pots had come down again. Monsieur Charles came out of the still-room and went along the passage leading to the street, after having glanced curiously at the superintendent. The women must have told him who he was.

He came back a few minutes later with an evening paper. It was a little after three. The women were washing up at the sink, up to their elbows in hot water.

Monsieur Charles however sat down at his little table and made himself as comfortable as possible. He spread out the paper, put on his glasses, lit a cigarette and began to read.

There was nothing odd about this, but Maigret was staring at him as though thunderstruck.

"Well," he said, smiling at Ramuel, who was counting his chits, "there's a break now, is there?"

"Until half past four, then it starts up again with the thé dansant . . ."

Maigret went on standing in the corridor for a short while longer. Then suddenly a bell rang in the still-room, Monsieur Charles got up, said a few words into the telephone, reluctantly left his paper and went off along the corridor.

"Where's he off to?"

"What time is it? Half past three? It's probably the store-keeper ringing him to give him his coffee and tea supplies."

"Does he do that every day?"

"Yes, every day . . ."

Ramuel watched Maigret, who was now calmly wander-ing into the still-room. He did nothing spectacular—merely opened the drawer of the table, which was an ordinary deal one. He found a small bottle of ink, a penholder and a packet of writing paper. There were also some stumps of pencils and two or three postal order counterfoils.

He was shutting the drawer when Monsieur Charles came back, carrying some packets. Seeing Maigret bend-ing over the table, he misinterpreted his action.

"You can take it . . ." he said, meaning the newspaper. "There's nothing in it! . . . I only read the serial and the small ads."

Maigret had guessed as much.

"There it was then . . . Prosper Donge sitting peacefully at his table . . . the three women over there splashing about in the sink . . . He . . ."

The superintendent was looking less and less ponder-ous and sleepy every minute. With the air of a man who has suddenly remembered that he has an urgent job to do, and without saying goodbye to anyone, he walked rapidly towards the cloakroom, seized his coat, put it on as he came out and a minute later had hurtled into a taxi.

"To the financial section of the Public Prosecutor's Department," he directed the driver.

A quarter to four. There might still be someone there. If all went well, there was a chance that by tonight . . . before the day was out . . .

He turned round. The taxi had just driven past Edgar Fagonet, alias Zebio, who was walking towards the Majestic.

10

DINNER AT THE COUPOLE

The operation was carried out with such brutal effective-ness that even an ancient antique dealer, rotting away at the back of his dark little shop like a mole, came to the door, dragging his feet over the floorboards.

It was a few minutes to six. The dingy shops in the Rue des Saints-Pères were feebly lit, and outside in the street there lingered a bluish twilight.

The police car shot round the corner with enough blasts on the horn to unnerve all the antique dealers and little shopkeepers in the street.

Then, with a squeal of brakes, it drew into the kerb, as three men jumped out, looking purposeful, as if summoned by an emergency call.

Maigret walked up to the door, alone, just as the pale, terrified face of a shop assistant came and glued itself to the glass, like a transfer. An inspector went up the side alley-way to check that the shop had no other entrance, and the policeman who remained on the pavement outside looked more like a caricature than a real inspector, with his large drooping moustache and baleful, suspicious eyes, for which reason he had been purposely chosen by Maigret.

In the shop, whose walls were hung with Persian carpets, giving it an air of opulent tranquillity, the assistant tried to appear calm.

"Did you want to see Monsieur Atoum? . . . I'll see if he's in . . ."

But the superintendent had already brushed the poor creature aside. He had spotted a glow of reddish light, coming from an opening in the carpets at the back of the shop, and could hear the murmur of voices. He found himself on the threshold of a small room, no bigger than a tent made of four carpets and furnished with a sofa covered with bright leather cushions, and a table inlaid with mother-of-pearl on which were cups of Turkish coffee.

A man had stood up and was about to leave, and seemed as ill at ease as the clerk. Another man was lying on the sofa smoking a gold-tipped cigarette, and said a few words in a foreign tongue.

"Monsieur Atoum, I believe? . . . Superintendent Maigret of the Judicial Police . . ."

The visitor hurriedly departed and there was a slam as the door of the shop closed behind him. Maigret sat himself composedly on the edge of the sofa, examining the little Turkish coffee cups with interest.

"Don't you recognize me, Monsieur Atoum? . . . We spent a whole half day together once, let me see . . . my goodness, it must be nearly eight years ago now . . . A splendid journey! . . . The Vosges, Alsace! If I remember rightly, we parted company near a frontier-post . . ."

Atoum was fat, but had a young face and magnificent eyes. He was richly dressed, with rings on his fingers, and

heavily scented, and reclined rather than sat on the sofa.
The small room, lit by a mock alabaster lamp, seemed more
like something in an Oriental bazaar than a Parisian street.

"Let me see—what was it you had done on that occasion? . . . Nothing much, as far as I can remember . . . But
as your papers weren't in order, the French Government
thought it would be a good idea to offer you a little trip
to the border . . . You came back that evening, of course,
but appearances were saved and I think you then found
protection . . ."

Atoum seemed quite unperturbed by all this, and
remained staring at Maigret with cat-like calm.

"After that you became a banker, because in France
you don't necessarily have to have a clean slate to handle
people's money . . . You've had various little difficulties
since, Monsieur Atoum . . ."

"May I be allowed to ask, superintendent . . ."

"What I'm doing here, you mean? Well, frankly, I don't
know. I've got a car and men outside. We may all go for a
little ride . . ."

Atoum's hand remained perfectly steady, as he lit a
cigarette, having offered one to Maigret, who refused.

"Or I could go peacefully off, leaving you here . . ."

"Depending on what?"

"The way you answer one small question . . . I know
how discreet you are, so I've taken a few precautions to
help you overcome this, as it were . . . When you were a
banker, you had a clerk who was your right-hand man,
your trusted confidant—you note I don't say accomplice—

called Jean Ramuel . . . Well—I'd like to know why you parted with such a trusted helper, why, to be more precise, you booted him out? . . ."

There was a long silence while Atoum reflected.

"You're mistaken, superintendent . . . I didn't get rid of Ramuel; he left of his own accord, for reasons of health, I think it was . . ."

Maigret got up.

"Too bad! In that case it'll have to be the first alternative . . . If you'd be good enough to come with me, Monsieur Atoum . . ."

"Where are you going to take me?"

"Back to the border . . ."

A smile hovered over the oriental's lips.

"But we'll try a different border this time . . . I think I'd like to make a little trip to Italy . . . I'm told that you left that country in undue haste and that you forgot to carry out a five-year sentence for forgery and passing counterfeit cheques . . . So . . ."

"Sit down, superintendent . . ."

"You think it won't be necessary for me to get up again in a hurry, then?"

"What do you want with Ramuel?"

"Perhaps to give him his deserts. What do you think?"

And changing his tone abruptly: "Come, Atoum! I've no time to waste today . . . I have no doubt Ramuel's got a hold over you . . ."

"I admit that if he were to talk inadvisedly, he could cause me a great deal of trouble. Banking affairs are com-

plex. He would stick his nose into everything . . . I wonder
if I wouldn't do better to choose Italy . . . Unless you can
give me some assurance . . . That if, for example, he speaks
of certain things, you won't pay any attention to them,
since that's all in the past and I'm now an honest businessman . . ."

"It's within the realm of possibility . . ."

"In that case I can tell you that Ramuel and I parted
company after a somewhat stormy exchange of words . . . I
had discovered, in fact, that he was working in my bank
on his own behalf, and that he had committed a number of
forgeries . . ."

"I suppose you kept the documents?"

Atoum batted his eyelids, and confessed in a whisper:
"But he has kept others, you see, so . . ."

"So you've got a mutual hold over each other . . .
Well, Atoum, I want you to give me those documents
immediately . . ."

He still hesitated. Italian or French prison? He finally
got up, and lifted the hanging behind the sofa, revealing a
little safe set in the wall, which he opened.

"Here are some bills of exchange on which Ramuel
copied, not only my signature, but also that of two of
my customers . . . If you find a little red book among his
things, in which I noted various transactions, I would be
grateful if you . . ."

And, as he crossed the shop after Maigret, he hesitated
a moment and then, pointing to a magnificent Kerman
carpet: "I wonder if Madame Maigret would like that
design . . ."

It was half past eight when Maigret walked into the Coupole and made for the part of the vast room where dinner was being served. He was alone, his hands in his pockets, as usual, and his bowler on the back of his head. He seemed to have nothing on his mind except looking for a free table.

Then he suddenly saw a small man already installed with a grill and a half of beer in front of him.

"Hello, Lucas! . . . Is this place free?"

He sat down at Lucas's table, smiling in anticipation at the thought of his dinner and then got up to give his coat to a waiter. An aggressive and common-looking woman sitting at the table next to him, with a half lobster of impressive dimensions, shouted in a disagreeable voice: "Waiter! . . . Bring some fresh mayonnaise . . . This smells of soap . . ."

Maigret turned towards her, and then to the man at her side, and said with a show of genuine astonishment: "Why—Monsieur Ramuel! . . . What a coincidence meeting you here! . . . Would you do me the honour of introducing? . . ."

"My wife . . . Superintendent Maigret, of the Judicial Police . . ."

"Delighted to meet you, superintendent . . ."

"Steak and chips, and a large beer, please, waiter!"

He glanced at Ramuel's plate, and saw that he was eating some noodles, without butter or cheese.

"Do you know what I think?" he said suddenly, in a friendly tone of voice. "It seems to me, Monsieur Ramuel, that you've always been unlucky . . . It struck me the first time I saw you . . . There are some people for whom nothing will go right, and I've noticed that it is just those same people who on top of all that fall prey to the most disagreeable illnesses and accidents . . ."

"He'll use what you say as an excuse for his horrible nature!" interrupted Marie Deligeard, sniffing the new mayonnaise she had just been brought.

"You're intelligent, well educated and hard-working," continued the superintendent, "and you should have made your fortune ten times over . . . And the strange thing is, that you nearly succeeded several times in gaining a marvellous position for yourself . . . In Cairo, for instance . . . Then in Ecuador . . . Each time, you had a rapid success, and then had to go right back to the beginning again . . . What happens when you get an excellent job in a bank? . . . You are unlucky enough to land up with a crooked banker—Atoum—and are obliged to leave . . ."

The people dining at the neighbouring tables had no idea what they were talking about. Maigret spoke in a cheerful, friendly tone of voice and attacked his steak with relish, while Lucas kept his nose buried in his plate and Ramuel appeared to be preoccupied with his noodles.

"In fact, I wasn't expecting to meet you here, in the Boulevard Montparnasse, as I thought you'd already be on the train to Brussels . . ."

Ramuel said nothing, but his face became even more yellow, and his fingers tightened on his fork. His companion shouted at him: "What? Hey—you were going to Brussels and hadn't said anything to me about it? What's up, Jean? . . . Another woman, eh?"

And Maigret said blandly: "I assure you, Madame, that it's got nothing to do with a woman . . . Don't worry . . . But your husband . . . I mean your friend . . ."

"You can call him my husband . . . I don't know what he's told you on that score, but we're well and truly married . . . I can prove . . ."

She fumbled frantically in her bag and pulled out a tightly folded, torn and faded bit of paper.

"There you are! . . . It's our marriage certificate . . ."

The text was in Spanish, and it was covered in Ecuadorian stamps and seals.

"Answer me, Jean! . . . What were you going to Brussels for?"

"But . . . I had no intention . . ."

"Come, Monsieur Ramuel . . . Forgive me—I had no intention of causing a family row . . . When I learnt that you had taken nearly all your money out of the bank and had asked for a cheque for two hundred and eighty thousand francs, to be drawn on Brussels . . ."

Maigret hurriedly bit into a mouthful of deliciously crisp chips, because he was having difficulty not to smile. A foot had been placed on his, and he realised it was Ramuel's—silently begging him to be quiet.

It was too late. Forgetting her lobster, forgetting the dozens of people dining round them, Marie Deligeard, or Madame Ramuel rather, if the bit of paper could be believed, shrieked: "Did you say two hundred and eighty thousand francs? . . . Do you mean he had two hundred and eighty thousand francs in the bank and kept me short? . . ."

Maigret looked pointedly at the lobster and half-bottle of twenty-five-franc Riesling . . .

"Answer me, Jean! . . . Is it true? . . ."

"I've no idea what the superintendent's talking about . . ."

"You've got a bank account?"

"I repeat, I haven't got a bank account, and if I did have two hundred and eighty thousand francs . . ."

"What do you mean by saying that, then, superintendent?"

"I'm so sorry, madame, to upset you like this. I thought you knew about it, that your husband hid nothing from you . . ."

"Now I understand!"

"What do you understand?"

"His attitude, recently . . . He was too kind . . . Fawning on me . . . But I thought it didn't seem natural . . . It was all part of the plan, wasn't it?"

People were turning to stare at them in amusement, because all this could be heard at least three tables away.

"Marie! . . ." Ramuel begged.

"You were making your pile in secret, were you, and letting me go without, while you got ready to leave . . . One fine day you'd have left, just like that! . . . I'd find myself all alone in a flat with the rent not even paid! . . . None of that, my little lad! . . . You've tried to sneak away twice already, but you know perfectly well it didn't work . . .

You're sure there's no woman tucked away somewhere, superintendent? . . ."

"Look, superintendent, don't you think it would be better if we continued this conversation somewhere else? . . ."

"No, no. Not a bit!" Maigret sighed. "Besides . . . I'd like . . . Waiter! . . ."

He pointed to the silver dish with a domed cover, which was being wheeled on a trolley between the tables.

"What have you got in your machine there?"

"A side of beef . . ."

"Good! Give me a slice, will you? A little beef, Lucas? . . . And some chips, please, waiter . . ."

"Take away my lobster—it's not fresh!" Ramuel's companion interrupted. "Give me the same as the superintendent . . . So the dirty beast had money tucked away all the time, and . . ."

She had become so heated she had to touch up her face, waving a doubtful pink powderpuff over the tablecloth.

And under the table, there was frantic activity—Ramuel quietly kicking her to make her shut up, and she pretending not to understand and stabbing him viciously with her heel in return.

"You'll pay for this, you beast! . . . Just you wait . . ."

"Look, I'll explain it all, in a minute . . . I don't know why the superintendent thinks . . ."

"And you, you're sure you're not mistaken? . . . I know what you police are like . . . When you can't find out anything and are floundering about in the dark, you invent something just to make people talk . . . I hope that's not what you're doing?"

Maigret looked at his watch. It was half past nine. He gave Lucas a quiet wink, and Lucas coughed. Then Maigret leant confidentially towards Ramuel and the woman.

"Don't move, Ramuel . . . Don't make a scene, it won't help . . . Your right-hand neighbour is one of our men . . . And Sergeant Lucas has been following you since this afternoon and it was he who telephoned me to let me know you were here . . ."

"What do you mean?" stuttered Marie Deligeard.

"I mean, madame, that I wanted to let you eat first . . . I'm afraid I have to put your husband under arrest . . . And it will be better for everyone if we do it quietly . . . Finish your meal . . . We'll go out together in a minute—all good friends . . . We'll get a taxi and go for a little ride to the Quai des Orfèvres . . . You can't imagine how peaceful the offices are at night . . . Some mustard, please, waiter! . . . And some gherkins, if you've got any . . ."

Marie Deligeard went on attacking her food with venom, giving her husband a terrible look from time to time, her brow furrowed with a deep scowl, which was hardly conducive to making her look any prettier or more prepossessing. Maigret ordered a third glass of beer and leant across to Ramuel, murmuring confidentially: "You see, at about four o'clock this afternoon, I suddenly remembered that you had been a quartermaster-sergeant . . ."

"You always said you were a second-lieutenant!" the odious woman spat, not missing a trick.

"But it's very smart, madame, being a quartermaster-sergeant! . . . It's the quartermaster-sergeant who does all the writing for the company . . . So, you see, I remembered my military service, which was a long time ago, as you can imagine . . ."

Nothing could prevent him enjoying his chips. They were sensational—crisp outside and melting within.

"As our captain came to the barracks as little as possible, it was our quartermaster-sergeant who signed all the passes and most other documents, in the captain's name, of course . . . And the signature was so well done that the captain could never tell which signatures he had written himself and which were the work of the quartermaster-sergeant . . . Do you see what I mean, Ramuel?"

"I don't understand . . . And as I imagine you're not going to try to arrest me without a proper warrant, I'd like to know . . ."

"I've got a warrant from the Financial Section of the Public Prosecutor's Department . . . Does that surprise you? . . . It happens quite often, you see . . . One is busy on a case . . . Without meaning to, one uncovers something else, which happened many years ago and which everyone has forgotten . . . I've got some bills in my pocket, given to me by a man called Atoum . . . You won't have any more to eat? . . . No dessert, madame? . . . Waiter! . . . We'll each pay for our own, don't you think? . . . What do I owe you, waiter? . . . I had a steak, something from the trolley, oh yes, some beef, three portions of chips and three beers . . . Have you got a light, Lucas?"

11

GALA EVENING AT POLICE HEADQUARTERS

The dark porch, then the great staircase, with a dim light at infrequent intervals, and finally the long corridor with its many doors.

Maigret said cheerfully to Marie Deligeard, who was out of breath: "We've arrived, madame . . . You can get your breath back . . ."

There was only one light on in the corridor, and two men were walking along deep in conversation—Oswald J. Clark and his solicitor.

At the end of the corridor was the waiting-room, which was glassed in on one side, to allow the police to come and watch their visitors if necessary. There was a table with a green cloth.

Green velvet armchairs. A Louis-Philippe clock on the mantelpiece—exactly like the one in Maigret's office and in no better working order. Black frames on the walls with photographs of policemen who had fallen on the field of glory.

Two women in armchairs, in a dark corner—Charlotte and Gigi.

In the corridor, on a bench, Prosper Donge—still without his tie and shoelaces—sitting between two policemen.

"This way, Ramuel! . . . Come into my office . . . And madame, would you be good enough to wait in the waiting-room for a minute, please? Will you show her the way, Lucas?"

He opened the door to his office. He was smiling at the thought of the three women left alone in the waiting-room, no doubt exchanging worried and angry glances.

"Come in, Ramuel! . . . You'd best take off your over-coat, because it looks as though we'll be here for some time . . ."

A green-shaded lamp on the table. Maigret took off his hat and coat, chose a pipe from his desk and opened the door of the inspectors' room.

It was as if Police Headquarters, usually so empty at night, had been stuffed with people for the occasion. Torrence was sitting at his desk, wearing a felt hat. He was smoking a cigarette, and sitting on a chair facing him was a little old man with a ragged beard, who was busily staring at his elastic-sided shoes.

Then there was Janvier who had seized the chance to write up his report, and who was keeping an eye on a middle-aged man, who looked like an ex-NCO.

"Are you the concierge?" Maigret asked him. "Would you come into my office for a minute?"

He stood aside to let him go in first. The man held his cap in his hand and didn't at first see Ramuel, who was standing as far from the light as possible.

"You're the concierge at 117b Rue Réaumur, aren't you? . . . Some time ago a man called Prosper Donge rented one of your offices and since then you have continued to send on his mail to him . . . Here . . . Do you recognize Donge?"

The concierge turned towards Ramuel in his corner, and shook his head, saying: "Hm . . . Er . . . Frankly . . . no! I can't say I do . . . I see so many people! . . . And it was three years ago, wasn't it? . . . I don't know if I remember rightly, but I have a vague idea that he had a beard . . . But perhaps the beard was someone else . . ."

"Thank you . . . You can go now . . . This way . . ."

One done. Maigret opened the door again and called: "Monsieur Jem! . . . I don't know what your real name is . . . Would you come in, please . . . And would you be good enough to tell me . . ."

There was no need to wait for an answer this time. The little old man started with surprise on seeing Ramuel.

"Well?"

"Well what?"

"Do you recognize him?"

The old man was furious.

"I'll have to go and give evidence at the trial, I suppose? And they'll leave me to rot for two or three days in the witnesses' room, and who'll look after my shop during that time? . . . Then, when I'm in the witness box I'll be asked a lot of embarrassing questions, and the lawyers will say a lot of things about me which will ruin my reputation . . . No thank you, superintendent!"

Then he suddenly added: "What's he done?"

"Well—he's killed two people for a start—a man and a woman . . . The woman was a rich American . . ."

"Is there a reward?"

"A pretty large one, yes . . ."

"In that case, you can write . . . I, Jean-Baptiste Isaac Meyer, businessman . . . Will there be many witnesses sharing the reward? . . . Because I know what happens . . . The police make fine promises . . . Then, when it comes to the point . . ."

"I'll write: '. . . *formally recognize in the man presented to me as Jean Ramuel the person with whom I dealt at my private correspondence bureau under the initials J. M. D. . . .*' Is that correct, Monsieur Meyer?"

"Where shall I sign?"

"Wait! I'll add: '. . . *And I confirm that the said person came to collect a final letter on . . .*' Now you can sign . . . You're a cunning old devil, Monsieur Meyer, because you know very well that all this will bring you a good deal of publicity and that everyone who hadn't already heard of your bureau will be rushing to contact you . . . Torrence! . . . Monsieur Meyer can go now . . ."

When the door had shut behind him, the superintendent read the repellent old man's statement with satisfaction. A voice made him start. It came from a dark corner of the room—only the lamp on the desk was lit.

"I protest, superintendent, you . . ."

Then Maigret suddenly seemed to remember that he had forgotten something. He began by pulling the unbleached cotton blind across the window. Then he looked at his hands. This was a Maigret that few people knew, and those who did, didn't often boast about it afterwards.

"Come here, my little Ramuel . . . Do as I say, come here!! . . . Farther! . . . Don't be afraid! . . ."

"What do . . . ?"

"You see, since I've discovered the truth, I've had a terrible desire to . . ."

As he spoke, Maigret's fist shot out and landed on the accountant's nose, as, too late, Ramuel raised his arm.

"There! . . . It's not really in order, of course, but it does one good . . . Tomorrow, the judge will interrogate you politely and everyone will be nice to you because you'll have become the star attraction of the court . . . Those gentlemen are always impressed by a star performer . . . If you see what I mean . . . There's some water in the basin, in the cupboard . . . Wash yourself, because you look disgusting like that . . ."

Ramuel, bleeding profusely, washed himself as well as he could.

"Let me see! . . . That's better! . . . You're almost pre-sentable . . . Torrence! . . . Lucas! Janvier! . . . Come on, lads . . . Bring in the ladies and gentlemen . . ."

Even his colleagues were surprised to find him much more elated than he usually was, even at the end of a difficult case. He had lit another pipe. The first to enter, between two policemen, was Donge, who held his hand-cuffed hands clumsily in front of him.

"Have you got the key?" Maigret asked one of the men.

He unlocked the handcuffs, and an instant later they snapped shut round Ramuel's wrists, while Donge stared at him with almost comic stupefaction.

The superintendent then noticed that Donge had neither tie nor shoelaces, and he ordered Ramuel's laces and his little black silk bow tie to be taken away.

"Come in, ladies . . . Come in, Monsieur Clark . . . I know you can't understand what we're saying . . . But I'm sure Monsieur Davidson will be kind enough to translate . . . Has everyone got a chair? . . . Yes, Charlotte, you can go and sit next to Prosper . . . But I must ask you not to be too effusive for the time being . . .

"Is everyone here? . . . Shut the door, Torrence!"

"What has he done?" Madame Ramuel asked in her coarse voice.

"Please sit down too, madame! . . . I hate talking to people who are standing up . . . No, Lucas! . . . Don't bother to put on the ceiling light . . . It's cosier like this . . . What has he done? . . . He's gone on doing what he's been doing all his life: committing forgeries . . . And I bet that if he's married you and spent so many years with a poisonous creature like you, saving your presence, it's because you've got a hold over him . . . And you've got a hold over him because you knew what he was up to in Guayaquil . . . There's a cable on its way there, and another for the company headquarters in London. I know in advance what the answer will be . . ."

And Marie chipped in in her vile voice: "Why don't you answer, Jean? . . . So the two hundred and eighty thousand francs and the trip to Brussels were true, then! . . ."

She had sprung up like a jack-in-the-box, and rushed towards him.

"Scoundrel! . . . Thief! . . . Scum! . . . To think . . ."

"Calm yourself, madame . . . It was much better that he didn't tell you anything because if he had done so, I would have been obliged to arrest you as an accomplice, not only in the forgery but in a double crime . . ."

From then on, an almost comic note was added to the proceedings. Clark, who kept his eyes on Maigret, kept leaning across to his solicitor to say a few words in English. Each time, the superintendent looked at him, and he was sure that the American must be saying, in his own language: "What's he saying?"

However, Maigret continued: "As for you, my poor Charlotte, I have to tell you something which Prosper perhaps told you on the last evening he spent with you . . . When you thought he was better and told him about Mimi's letter and the story of the child, he wasn't better at all . . . He didn't say anything, but set to work during the rest period, in his still-room, as Ramuel has explained, writing a long letter to his old mistress . . .

"Don't you remember, Donge? . . . Don't you remember the details?"

Donge didn't know what to reply. He couldn't understand what was going on and kept looking round him with his great sky-blue eyes.

"I don't understand what you mean, sir . . ."

"How many letters did you write?"

"Three . . ."

"And on at least one of the three occasions, weren't you disturbed by a telephone call? . . . Weren't you summoned to go to the storekeeper to collect your rations for the next day? . . ."

"Possibly . . . Yes . . . I think I probably was . . ."

"And your letter stayed on your table, just opposite Ramuel's booth . . . Unlucky Ramuel's booth . . . Ramuel who, all his life long, has committed forgeries without ever winning a fortune . . . Who did you give your letters to to take them to the post?"

"The lift-boy . . . He took them up to the hall, where there was a postbox . . ."

"So Ramuel could easily have intercepted them . . . And Mimi . . . Forgive me, Monsieur Clark . . . She is still Mimi to us . . . After Mrs. Clark, I should say, had received some letters from her ex-lover, in Detroit, in which he wrote mainly about his son, she then received other, more menacing letters, in the same handwriting and still signed Donge . . . But these letters demanded money . . . The new Donge wanted to be paid to keep silent . . ."

"Oh sir! . . ." cried Prosper.

"Be quiet, man! . . . and for the love of God try to understand! . . . Because it's all very complex, I assure you . . . And it's proof yet again that Ramuel never had any luck . . . First he had to write to Mimi that you had changed your address, which was easy, because you hadn't said much in your letters about your new way of life . . . Then he rented the office in the Rue Réaumur in the name of Prosper Donge . . ."

"But . . ."

"There is no need of any proof of identity to rent an office and you are given any mail which arrives addressed to you . . . Unfortunately the cheque Mimi sent was made out to Prosper Donge, and banks do ask for your papers to be in order . . .

"I repeat that Ramuel is an artist in that line . . . But first of all he had to know that you would be having half to three-quarters of an hour off, in the still-room, opposite his glass booth, under his very eyes, so to speak, and that you would spend the break writing your letters . . .

"He suddenly sees you writing a letter to your bank to close your account and asking them to send the balance to Saint-Cloud . . .

"But it wasn't this letter which reached the Crédit Lyonnais. It was another letter, written by Ramuel, still in your handwriting, merely giving a change of address . . . In future, any letters to Donge were to be addressed to 117b Rue Réaumur . . .

"Then the cheque is sent in . . . To be paid into the account . . . As for the eight-hundred-odd francs that you got in Saint-Cloud, it was Ramuel who sent them to you in the bank's name . . .

"A cleverly worked out bit of dirty business, as you can see! . . .

"So clever in fact that Ramuel, distrusting the address in the Rue Réaumur, took the additional precaution of having his post sent to a box number . . .

"Who would be able to get on his tracks now?

"Then suddenly, the unexpected happened . . . Mimi

comes to France . . . Mimi is staying at the Majestic . . . Any minute now, Donge, the real Donge, may meet her and tell her that he has never tried to blackmail her, and . . ."

Charlotte couldn't take any more. She was crying, without quite knowing why, as she might have done when reading a sad story or seeing a sentimental film. Gigi whispered in her ear: "Don't! . . . Don't! . . ."

And no doubt Clark was still mumbling to his solicitor: "What's he saying?"

"As for Mrs. Clark's death," Maigret continued, "it was accidental . . . Ramuel, who had access to the hotel register, knew she was at the Majestic . . . Donge didn't know this . . . He learnt of it by chance on overhearing a conversation in the guests' servants' hall . . .

"He wrote to her . . . He fixed a rendezvous for six in the morning and probably wanted to demand that he should be given his son, beg her on his knees, beseech her . . . I'm sure that if they had met, Mimi would have run rings round him again . . .

"He didn't know that, thinking she was about to meet a blackmailer, she had bought a gun . . .

"Ramuel was worried. He didn't leave the Majestic basement. The little note Donge had sent via a bellboy had escaped his notice . . .

"And there it was! . . . A punctured tyre . . . Donge is a quarter of an hour late . . . Ramuel sees the young woman wandering along the corridor in the basement and guesses what has happened, and is afraid that everything will come out . . .

"He strangles her . . . Pushes her in a locker . . .

"He soon realizes that everything will point to Donge, and that there is nothing, in fact, which could possibly incriminate him . . .

"To make doubly certain of this, he writes an anonymous letter, in Charlotte's handwriting . . . Because there are several notes from Charlotte in the drawer in the still-room . . .

"I repeat, he's a consummate artist! Meticulous! . . . He takes care of every detail! . . . And when he realizes that poor Justin Colleboeuf has seen him . . . When Colleboeuf comes to tell him that he feels duty bound to denounce him to the police, he commits another crime, with no trouble at all, and one which can easily be attributed to Donge . . .

"That is all . . . Torrence! . . . Use a damp towel on that scum—his nose is beginning to bleed again . . . He slipped just now and banged his face on the corner of the table . . .

"Have you anything to say, Ramuel?"

Silence. Only the American was still asking: "What's he saying?"

"As for you, madame . . . What shall I call you? . . . Marie Deligeard? . . . Madame Ramuel? . . ."

"I prefer Marie Deligeard . . ."

"That's what I thought . . . You weren't mistaken in thinking he hoped to leave you soon . . . No doubt he was waiting until there was a nice round sum in the bank . . . Then he could go and look after his liver abroad, alone, a long way from your ranting and raving . . ."

"No!"

"With all due respect, madame! . . . with all due respect! . . ."

And suddenly: "Constables . . . Take the prisoner to the cells . . . I hope that tomorrow examining magistrate Bonneau will be good enough to sign a warrant and that . . ."

Gigi was standing in a corner, perched on her stilt-like legs, and all the emotion had given her such a craving for drugs that she felt dizzy, and her nostrils fluttered like a wounded bird's wings.

"Excuse me, superintendent . . ."

It was the solicitor. Clark stood behind him.

"My client would like there to be a meeting between you, Monsieur Donge and himself, in my office, as soon as possible, to discuss . . . discuss the child who . . ."

"D'you hear that, Prosper?" cried Gigi triumphantly, from her corner.

"Would tomorrow morning suit you? . . . Are you free tomorrow morning, Monsieur Donge? . . ."

But Donge couldn't speak. He had suddenly cracked. He had thrown himself on Charlotte's ample bosom and was crying, crying his heart out, as the saying goes, while, a little embarrassed, she soothed him like a child.

"Pull yourself together, Prosper! . . . We'll bring him up together! . . . We'll teach him French . . . We'll . . ."

Maigret—God knows why—was rummaging through the drawers of his desk. He remembered that he had put some little sachets he had taken during a recent raid in one of them. He took a sachet out, hesitated a moment, and then shrugged.

Then, as Gigi was almost fainting, he brushed past her. His hand touched hers.

"Ladies and gentlemen, it's one o'clock . . . If you'll be so good . . ."

"*What's he saying*," Clark seemed still to be asking, at the end of his first encounter with the French police.

————

They learnt the following morning that the cheque for two hundred and eighty thousand francs had been presented at the Société Générale in Brussels, by a man called Jaminet, who was a bookmaker by trade.

Jaminet had received it by airmail from Ramuel, under whose command he had been when he was doing his military service, as a corporal.

Which didn't prevent Ramuel denying everything to the last.

Or from being lucky for the first time in his life, because owing to his poor state of health—he fainted three times during the final hearing—his death sentence was commuted to transportation with hard labour for life.